Ryan stopped short

when he saw the figure curled up asleep on the sofa. A twinge of guilt seized him. Valerie had every right to be tired. She was the chief executive of a small but thriving company, and instead of relaxing this weekend she was at his house playing hostess.

He tried to tell himself it was merely sympathy that kept his feet rooted to the floor. He knew how tired she must be, and he hated to wake her.

But then realism and honesty prevailed. A host of emotions were raging within him at the sight of her lying there, but sympathy certainly wasn't among them....

Dear Reader,

Welcome to the Silhouette **Special Edition** experience! With your search for consistently satisfying reading in mind, every month the authors and editors of Silhouette **Special Edition** aim to offer you a stimulating blend of deep emotions and high romance.

The name Silhouette **Special Edition** and the distinctive arch on the cover represent a commitment—a commitment to bring you six sensitive, substantial novels each month. In the pages of a Silhouette **Special Edition**, compelling true-to-life characters face riveting emotional issues—and come out winners. Both celebrated authors and newcomers to the series strive for depth and dimension, vividness and warmth, in writing these stories of living and loving in today's world.

The result, we hope, is romance you can believe in. Deeply emotional, richly romantic, infinitely rewarding—that's the Silhouette **Special Edition** experience. Come share it with us—six times a month!

From all the authors and editors of Silhouette **Special Edition**,

Best wishes,

Leslie Kazanjian,
Senior Editor

ANDREA EDWARDS
Violets Are Blue

Silhouette Special Edition

Published by Silhouette Books New York

America's Publisher of Contemporary Romance

Books by Andrea Edwards

Silhouette Special Edition

Rose in Bloom #363
Say It with Flowers #428
Ghost of a Chance #490
Violets Are Blue #550

Silhouette Intimate Moments

Above Suspicion #291

ANDREA EDWARDS

is the pseudonym of Anne and Ed Kolaczyk, a husband-and-wife team who concentrate on women's fiction. "Andrea" is a former elementary schoolteacher, while "Edwards" is a refugee from corporate America, having spent almost twenty-five years selling computers before becoming a full-time writer in 1982. They have four children, two dogs and four cats and live in South Bend, Indiana, in an old home on the edge of the University of Notre Dame campus.

Roses are red,
Violets are blue,
Your kids are brats.
I quit! I'm through!
        —Mrs. H.P.D., former housekeeper
            for the Crawfords

Roses are red,
Violets are blue,
We weren't really bad,
Just played a joke or two.
        —Casey (13), Robert (10)
            and Richard (10) Crawford

Roses are red,
Violets are blue,
No need to panic,
HSI will find the right housekeeper for you.
        —Valerie Dennison,
            owner of Home Services, Inc.

Chapter One

Ah, Miss Dennison, good afternoon. What a pleasure to see you again."

"Hello, Maurice."

M.C. Jones had purchased Jouberts, Fort Wayne's finest continental restaurant, about ten years ago. The word on the street had it that he'd gotten the money from the horses, the name from a dead French actor, and the accent from Berlitz, but Valerie Dennison didn't pay the rumors any mind. The food was good and she made it a point never to pry into anyone's past. Control was what counted, control of one's life and one's destiny. Yesterday mattered only if one let it dictate today and tomorrow.

"You are here to meet Ryan Crawford, correct?" Maurice asked. "Unfortunately Mr. Crawford is still at his office. Would you like to wait in the bar or perhaps with the children? Their grandfather brought them a few minutes ago.''

Val looked through the doorway at the table toward which he was gesturing. Three children stared back at her. Neatly scrubbed, formally dressed and solemn faced. She hesitated a moment. What was it their former housekeeper had said when Val had called for some background on the family? Don't go near those kids unless you have a whip or an armed guard, preferably both. But then, they were the reason Val was here. To find them the perfect housekeeper from among all those listed with her service.

"I'll wait with the children." She forced a smile to her lips. "It'll give us a chance to get better acquainted."

"Don't look so worried when you say that," Maurice scolded. "I've known the family for years and they haven't eaten me yet."

"They save their terrors only for their housekeepers, is that it?"

"And you aren't a housekeeper, are you?"

Val followed him to the table, doubts washing over her with each step she took, in spite of his gentle scolding. Maybe she should have waited for the father to arrive. What did she know about talking to kids? Especially ones who had run wild since their mother died of cancer a year and a half ago, ones that went through housekeepers like Val went through pantyhose. But it was too late to turn back without looking ridiculous, or worse, chicken. She squared her shoulders as they stopped at the table.

"Casey." Maurice bowed to the pretty, blue-eyed girl with reddish hair. "This is Miss Dennison. Your father is expecting her."

"Oh, yes," the young teenager exclaimed as an eager smile spread across her face. "Won't you please sit down? I'm Casey Crawford."

"Hello," Val said cautiously as she sat down. The children had been described as hellions but they looked like perfect little angels. Val took a deep breath, trying to present a relaxed exterior as she—per instructions from another housekeeper—kept all three children in her line of sight.

"These are my twin brothers," Casey said. "Richard and Robert."

Clean faces under slicked down hair flashed glowing smiles at Val. The boys were mirror images of each other, exact duplicates, and Val could immediately see what fun that would be for a housekeeper. How in the world did anyone tell them apart?

"Which one of you is Richard and which one is Robert?

The twins silently pointed at each other. Big help.

"Richard wears the red tie," Casey hurriedly explained. "And Robert wears the blue tie."

Val looked back at the boys and they nodded vigorously.

"Do you guys speak?" Val asked.

They nodded.

"Good." Val was losing the battle and they were winning it. She knew she should have met with the father in her office rather than accepting his invitation to lunch. Maurice's spinach salad was great, but so was a carton of yogurt eaten in peace and quiet at her desk. She took a sip of her water.

"Well," she said, clearing her throat and looking at her watch. "It looks like your father is late."

"He's always late," Casey said, rolling her eyes heavenward.

"Grandma said he was born late," the red-tied twin said.

"Yup," the blue tie agreed. "And Grandpa said he'll be late to his own funeral."

"That should pretty much cover everything," Val said, as she looked rapidly from one twin to the other. Which one was Richard and which one was Robert?

"Actually I'm just as happy that father is late." Casey hitched her chair over closer to Val, who successfully fought the urge to move back. "It presents us with an excellent opportunity to become better acquainted."

Val closely examined the three faces moving in on her. She'd dearly love a glass of wine but felt she needed a clear head, not to mention a chair and whip. "Yes," she agreed. "It certainly does."

"Miss Dennison." Casey folded her hands on the table in front of her. "We desperately need your assistance."

"Oh?" For thirteen, this girl was pretty well-spoken. She acted like she was thirteen going on thirty. Then Val's heart softened. Things couldn't have been easy for the girl in the past year and that tended to make you older, no matter what the calendar said. You learned, if nothing else, to put on a good front and pretend control. Val knew that better than most people.

"You absolutely must find us the best, no, the most perfect housekeeper in the whole world," Casey told her. "If you don't—" the girl looked at her brothers and they in turn looked at each other "—our father will secure us the services of a mother."

Val shook her head. "I'm afraid I don't understand what the problem is," she said. "I thought that was why

I'm here, to discuss the type of housekeeper your father wants."

The girl sighed. "We've had the type of housekeeper Father wants before." The boys nodded in unison. "They didn't work out very well."

"As I understood it, the three of you aren't exactly a cup of tea for a housekeeper," Val pointed out.

But Casey put a brave look in her eye and clasped her hands even more tightly. "I admit that at times we didn't have the best of attitudes," Casey said. "But what you have to understand, Miss Dennison, is that we had a great deal of grief to work through. We loved our mother dearly."

The twins stared at Val as mixed feelings danced in her heart. Casey was telling the truth. Val knew that losing a parent was not an easy thing. There seemed to be no way to fight that lost, frightened feeling. Time helped, if you were surrounded by love, but if you were alone...

Val shook her head, vowing not to let her past cloud her perception of the trio at the table. Sure the kids had suffered, but they also were con artists and she wasn't going to be taken for a ride. "So..." she began,

"So I wanted you to know that's all behind us now." Casey forced an extra hundred watts of brightness into her smile. "The task we have at hand is to get a good housekeeper and make sure Father doesn't do anything foolish."

Val put a smile on her own lips. "Foolish?"

"Father chose all the other housekeepers himself by running ads in the paper or hiring friends of friends. They were not at all particularly qualified. Lately we think he's been considering another option," Casey said.

"He started dating again," Richard said. Robert nodded his affirmation.

"And Father's choice of companions has been rather poor."

"Real dogs," Robert said.

"Personalitywise," Richard assured her.

Val twirled her water glass with her fingers. So the twins really *did* speak. "And where does this fit in with his hiring my service to find a housekeeper?" she asked.

"When our last housekeeper left—" Casey began.

"There was an illness in her family," one boy pointed out.

"We didn't do anything," the other added.

That wasn't what Val had heard, but she didn't get a chance to say anything before Casey spoke up again.

"Anyway," the girl said quickly, "things changed when Mrs. Pendalski left. We think this is our last chance. If you can't find us the right housekeeper, we think he's going to marry just to provide us with a mother."

The two boys nodded solemnly.

"Oh, Miss Dennison." Casey's expression turned so sincere Val thought she'd overdose on the sweetness in the air. "All we really need is a housekeeper. Just an adult to oversee the minutiae of our day-to-day life."

Again the boys just nodded.

Val looked at all three of them, eyes wide and innocent, sincerity flowing down their faces like chocolate fudge on a sundae. She would have given her life's savings for a slice of lemon right at that moment. But maybe she hadn't lost control of this situation after all.

"Well, my little dears," Val said with the barest of smiles, "it looks like you guys are up the proverbial creek without a paddle. You can't afford to send another housekeeper screaming for the hills, can you?"

"Those days of trauma and immaturity are behind us, Miss Dennison. Of that I can assure you."

"I guess you'd better make sure of it," Val said, but then suddenly the girl's face softened and lit up in a natural joy as she sprang up from her chair.

"Daddy," Casey cried. She flew into the arms of a tall, good-looking man who was approaching the table. His dark hair was sprinkled sparingly with gray; his arms closed around Casey briefly.

"Hi, honey," he said, then went around the table to the boys and patted each on the shoulder. "Hi, guys."

"Hi, Dad," they chorused.

So this was Ryan Crawford. Val watched as he greeted his children, affection riding visibly in his dark eyes. He was in his early forties and either exercised regularly and with vigor or was blessed with a naturally perfect physique. Not that he was picture perfect handsome. No, Val would have found that reason enough for distrust, but he was easy on the eyes with an aura of comfort about him.

Comfortable. Yes, that was the word to describe Ryan Crawford. There was something very comfortable about him. Maybe it was his summer suit, made of a dark nubby fabric that didn't have the pressed and formal look of most business apparel. Maybe it was his eyes that seemed ready, willing and able to laugh. Or maybe it was his smile, warm and easy, and which, when aimed at her, made her feel like he truly was glad to see her.

"Hello," he said, making his way around the table to take her hand. "I'm Ryan Crawford. Sorry I'm late, but I got tied up with a call."

Richard snickered. Robert wiggled around vigorously as if someone had a rope around his arms. Ryan tossed them a glaring glance that returned them both quickly to a state of decorum.

"Well," Ryan said, as he sat down. "It looks like you all have had a chance to get acquainted."

"Yes, Father, we certainly have," Casey said, the boys nodding their agreement even though Ryan wasn't looking at them.

"I even know who's who," Val said. "Richard has the red tie and Robert has the blue one."

Ryan looked sharply at the twins. "Yes, that's right."

His eyes came back to Val's, his smile just a touch warmer, as if saying she was different, better than the rest who'd been fooled by their appearances. Her lips were tempted to smile back and she did, but knew it wasn't felt in her heart. Friendships, even business friendships, were best kept at bay, but putting up a good front was something she could do with expertise.

"Did you get the tickets for the dog show?" Casey asked.

Ryan turned to his daughter. "I got the tickets but I'm afraid your Aunt Sarah will be taking you, not me."

"Aunt Sarah," Robert moaned. "She makes us all hold hands so we won't get lost."

"Why can't Grandma and Grandpa take us?" Richard asked.

"They're already on their way to Indianapolis with Grandma's garden club," Casey said, then turned to her father. "I thought you were going to take the afternoon off so we could all go together."

Ryan just shrugged his apology. "Something came up and I'm not going to be able to take the time off. I have to get back to the office soon. How about if Miss Dennison and I talk for a while and get the business all done? Then we can all have a leisurely lunch before your aunt comes."

The boy's faces fell while Casey put on a mask of affability. "Certainly, Father."

Ryan took a sip from the glass of water before him. To Val he appeared to be a charming man with a friendliness that seemed natural, not practiced. It was, no doubt, something that helped him immensely in his business life. But he also seemed to have blinders on. What was the big deal about sparing an afternoon for your children?

He leaned forward in his chair, turning so that he was facing Val. "My need for a housekeeper is fairly immediate," he said. "Now that school is out, the kids have been spending their days with their grandparents."

"Grandpa and Grandma are nice." Robert's words were emphasized by Richard's vigorous nodding.

"Yes, they are," Ryan agreed, smiling over at his son. "But they don't have the energy to keep up with you guys, and besides, they have plans that will keep them in the city for most of the summer."

He returned his attention to Val. "We've had some rough times over the past year," he said. "So when a friend offered us the use of his cottage at Long Lake for the summer, I jumped at the chance. I want the kids to spend the summer up there just lazing around, like kids are supposed to."

"Why don't you laze around with us, Dad?" Casey had suddenly dropped her teenage affectations like an old coat.

"Honey, we've been all through this already. Things are turning real busy for me now." He turned to Val with a weak smile. "As I told you on the phone I'm a professional fund-raiser," he explained. "I help colleges and other not-for-profit organizations stay alive. When the kids' mother died I stayed home most of the time, producing a newsletter, dispensing advice over the telephone, and that kind of thing. But my clients need more of me now and I want to give it.''

His comfortable style somehow didn't detract from the sense of energy and enthusiasm in him just waiting to explode, and Val guessed that he'd be happier dashing around. Not that he didn't care about his kids. Anyone could see he did. But did he really understand what they needed and wanted? She frowned, forcing her attention back to his words.

"What I really need is a good, solid housekeeper. Someone I can leave the kids with while I'm on business trips or working here in the city. She needs to cook a little bit, keep the house reasonably neat, but most of all she has to manage the kids so that they have fun without any harm coming to them.''

The business woman in her took over. "You keep saying 'she'," Val said. "Does that mean you'd object to a male housekeeper?''

Ryan blinked in confusion. "No, I just thought—'' Val could see him searching for the right words. "I just thought that housekeepers were usually women.''

"They usually are," Val replied. "I just wanted to see if you had any strong preferences, one way or the other.''

"No.'' He shook his head vigorously. "Not at all. Right now I'm willing to consider anyone capable.''

Val looked at him more closely, seeing a hint of a shadow in his eyes. Hidden behind the laughter and affability was weariness and something else that she couldn't read.

Val frowned to herself. Reading her customer's unspoken needs as well as his spoken ones was part of her success, yet she was getting mixed signals from Ryan Crawford. She pushed ahead gently. "You've had a number of housekeepers already," she pointed out.

Ryan Crawford looked down at the table for a long moment, a thoughtful expression on his face. "Yes, we have," he said slowly. "I know it doesn't look good, but I guess we just haven't had the right matchups. I guess the personal karmas were opposed or something like that."

Personal karmas? Val silently groaned. "As I understand it, your children are difficult to deal with."

He looked quickly at the serious young faces studying his. Would he stand with them or against them? Val wondered.

"There were some problems," Ryan admitted. "But the housekeepers I hired were less than flexible."

Ryan had found a middle ground, doling out the blame in equal portions. So he saw his kids realistically, but also loved them and wasn't about to give them all the blame. He seemed a straightforward, caring single parent who needed help to cope with everything. Why had she sensed there was something else?

"Your service comes highly recommended, Miss Dennison."

Val glanced briefly at him. "Thank you."

It ought to. It was her life and she'd worked hard to make it as successful as it was. After her college education had become sidetracked, she'd gotten a job as a maid in a hotel, moving up in the housekeeping ranks and occasionally taking other part-time household jobs herself or finding someone else willing to perform them from among the hotel staff. That way she'd started her service almost without knowing it. Eight years ago she'd quit the hotel to run the service full-time, eventually expanding from a provider of maids to a total household service. She had employees who would do everything from cleaning houses to walking the dog to stocking the freezer. Her motto was, if a home needed the service, she'd find someone to do it. Just as she'd find the right person to keep the Crawford household in line.

"Well, you obviously know a good deal about us by now," Ryan said. "Think you can find us that very special person we need? How many tough, gentle and flexible housekeepers do you have available?"

"Enough," Val said. "And maybe even one or two who can walk on water."

But before Ryan could say anything a well-dressed, young blonde swayed over to their table. "Oh, Mr. Crawford, I'm so glad I found you."

"Yes, Lisa?"

"The Kidney Foundation called. They have to re-schedule your meeting to this coming Thursday, but Dan says that's impossible because the patient survey won't be back until then."

"Damn." Ryan got to his feet with a quick apologetic glance around the table. "I'm afraid I'll have to take care of this." He glanced at the children. "I'll tell Maurice that you'll be staying here until your aunt comes. Order whatever you want. I'll settle with him later."

A single look was all that Val needed to see the disappointment in the children's eyes. And that was all it had taken to see briefly into Ryan Crawford's soul. For a split second as he'd stood up from the table, Val had seen uncertainty in his eyes. For all his talk, he wasn't sure that a housekeeper was what was needed. Were the children right in suspecting he was considering marrying to provide them with a mother? What kind of relationship would that be for any of them?

Val took a deep breath and tried to fight back the cloud of depression that wanted to settle over the table as Ryan left. "Well, I'm starved. Let's order," she said, forcing a cheerfulness into her voice as she signaled for the waitress.

Casey nodded, her face wearing a mask once more. "I thought that was a productive meeting," she said. "Do you have a better idea of our requirements now?"

Val turned back to them, examining the three faces in front of her. Loneliness peeked around edges of toughness and veneers of sophistication. They needed to be hugged and swatted and loved. She doubted that she would be able to find what they really needed, but she would do her best to come close.

"Yes, I do," she assured them.

Chapter Two

I am not a marine sergeant, Mr. Crawford. Chocolate chip cookies are my specialty, not cracking a whip.''

Mrs. Staples's words and the subsequently slammed door echoed and reechoed to all the far cracks and crevasses of Ryan's mind until anger was the only defense he had left. He stalked into the kitchen. The smell of the cookies that was still hanging in the air stoked his anger higher. He knew he'd explained to that woman what they needed and she'd sent over a grandmother substitute. The kids already had a grandmother.

He strode into the dining room, then the living room. The sofa pillows were still scattered over the floor from the pillow fight. He picked them up slowly. He'd told Valerie they needed somebody tough and responsible, and she'd given them Mrs. Claus, straight from the North Pole.

He walked out onto the porch, skirting the white wicker furniture to stand at the window and stare out at the garden, green and vibrant in the June sunlight. Normally every jangled nerve in his system would be soothed by staring at the outdoor scene, but not today. Not when he was called out of an important organizational meeting to rescue the besieged Mrs. Staples. Not when he was consumed with guilt for leaving the kids in the first place. Not when he was doubting that their lives would ever return to a near-normal state.

The hall clock chimed and Ryan stomped back into the house to compare his watch to the clock. Where in the world was that woman? She'd sent him an absolute disaster of a housekeeper and now she couldn't even come out to the house to see the damage her employee had wrought.

It was imperative that she see for herself what happened when the kids were left with someone who couldn't control them. Ryan didn't want her making the same mistake twice. He looked at his watch again and shook his head. Hells bells, by the time that woman got here, the kids would have the shaving cream cleaned up from their bedrooms.

Suddenly exhaustion overcame him and Ryan slumped down onto the bottom step of the curved stairway that led upstairs. He didn't understand it. He'd thought they were all healed, he'd thought life should start moving ahead and they should all stop clinging to each other. What had gone wrong? He rubbed his eyes tiredly. He could understand the boys getting into that kind of mischief, but Casey? Casey had been growing into a young lady. He'd been starting to depend on her.

Psychology had never been an interest of his, but he knew enough to know that the sudden mischievousness of his children was something more than youthful high spirits. If it had started up soon after Maggie's death, he'd have thought it was a reaction to the natural feeling of abandonment they all went through. But it hadn't. It had taken more than a year to surface. A year when they were totally under his care. So it was all his fault? He didn't like that line of reasoning.

He shook his head wearily. Being a father with a mother around hadn't been all that hard, but the dual role of father/mother was almost too much for him.

"Damn it," he swore through clenched teeth as he jumped to his feet. "Where is that woman?" If she didn't get here soon he was going to—

The musical chimes of the front door interrupted his train of threats. He strode to the door and jerked it open.

"Good evening," Val said, easily carrying the glow of the early evening sun in her short, light brown hair. Her gray eyes were as serene as a becalmed lake at dusk.

His psyche leaped up and smashed all feelings of softness within him. "You're late," he said, pointing at his watch and expecting her to be flustered or even irritated by his remark. What he hadn't expected was her sweet, gentle smile.

"I'm sorry," she said. "Am I trespassing on your territory?"

Warmth moved up from his neck and on into his cheeks. Ryan quickly clenched his teeth hoping to squelch the display of any emotion except irritation.

"Come in," he snapped.

"Certainly," Val replied, still wearing her easy smile. "What lady could refuse such a lovely invitation?"

His conscience reached out and pinched him. "I'm sorry," he said, though his voice was still tight with tension. "I haven't had a good day, not by the loosest of definitions."

"So I heard."

"I see," he said. "Mrs. Staples has already given you her side of the story."

"I don't see that the story has any sides to it," Val said. "Your kids have acted up again."

"My kids." Anger, defeat and guilt rolled around and wrestled within him. "So it's all the kids' fault?"

Val rolled her eyes toward the ceiling. "I didn't say that." She glared at him a moment. "If we're going to assign fault around here, I'd give *you* most of it."

"Me?"

"Look," she snapped, "I've had a hard day too. If you want to argue I'd like to do it someplace more comfortable than standing around in your foyer. Do you have some place nice where we can sit down?"

"Yes." Irritation rose, but he was no longer absolutely certain just what he was irritated about. "The porch is very nice."

They stood still for several moments, glaring at each other until finally Val broke the silence, speaking very quietly. "Can I sit there or is it off-limits?"

By now his irritation was turning inward. Ryan wondered if his good manners had vanished along with the order that his life used to contain. He nodded and silently led the way to the back.

"This is beautiful." He heard the words behind and turned to see Val looking out at the yard. He saw rapture in her eyes.

"Yeah, it is. We have a great gardener. Retired guy just down the street. He does it to keep busy and because he loves gardens."

"It shows," she replied.

"The daylilies will bloom in another few weeks," he said. "Then you'll really see beautiful."

She looked at him and laughed. "Is that an invitation?"

Caught unawares, Ryan blinked, then shrugged. "If you want to take it that way."

"Your charm is rather overwhelming. I'd better wait until my heart settles down before I make a decision concerning your invitation."

Ryan decided to quit while he was still in one piece. "Why don't you sit down and relax while I get us something to drink?" he said. "Would you like alcoholic or non?"

"Non."

Fortunately the kids hadn't drunk, or spilled, all the lemonade in the refrigerator. He poured two glasses over ice. When he returned, Val had her shoes off and her feet on a wicker ottoman.

"You said to relax," she said with just a touch of defiance to sweeten her tone.

"Take off as much as you want." Val blushed and this time it was his turn to laugh.

They sat, sipped their cool drinks and looked out over the garden. A surprising feeling of ease and comfort descended over Ryan.

He sat forward in his chair. "I thought we needed to talk things over face-to-face," he said, interrupting his own thoughts before they went too far.

"Okay." She turned her attention back to him, open and honest eyes giving him a level stare.

Ryan looked down into his drink for a moment. "I don't want to sound like an old grouch," he started. "But I think I know what my kids need. I certainly know what they don't need. They don't need to be spoiled and smothered to death.''

Val took a sip of her drink. She was a very calm and collected woman and that sense of relaxation seemed to spread to him. He felt some of the tension leave the back of his neck.

''We've had enough smothering,'' he said, his tone softening. ''When kids lose a mother all kinds of strange people come out of the woodwork. People who want the kids to stay sad and helpless so that they can minister to them and feel important.''

She still hadn't said anything and Ryan looked at her. ''Am I making any kind of sense?''

Val nodded. ''Some.''

There was something in her eyes that he couldn't read, but before he could try, it was gone. He went on. ''They're just regular kids, full of life, and they need to be treated like regular kids. Most of all they need discipline.''

Val didn't reply immediately. She just jiggled the ice cubes about in her glass, staring down into it.

''I don't mean a marine drill sergeant,'' he said, remembering Mrs. Staples's parting words. ''What I'd like is a stern, but loving wo—person.'' He smiled. ''Sort of like a lot of school teachers I had in my day.''

''If you remember any names, just give them to me,'' Val said. ''I'll be glad to check them out.''

Ryan shook his head. ''I've tried everything.''

''I'll keep looking.''

She put her glass down on a pile of magazines that covered the tabletop and Ryan felt a sudden, aching need to keep her there. Somehow she'd been holding back the chaos. Just the quiet calm of her presence was enough to convince him that normality was attainable.

"Sometimes I wonder if it's just us," he said. "Maybe we really are too much trouble."

Val shrugged. "I wouldn't know. I don't know your family that well."

"Maybe you should," Ryan replied. "Stay for dinner. We ordered a pizza and it'll be here soon."

"Thank you, but that's not necessary. I'll just keep looking for a housekeeper and we'll see what comes of it."

He stood up with her as Casey came onto the porch, followed by her partners in crime.

"Miss Dennison. Hi."

"Hello, Casey. Hello, Richard. Hello, Robert." Val nodded in the twins' general direction. They were dressed alike in green T-shirts and navy blue shorts and Ryan would have given only fifty-fifty odds that Val could tell them apart. But she was treating them as individuals which was more than a lot of other people did.

"Are you staying for dinner?" Casey asked. "You haven't eaten yet, have you?"

"No, but I really have to go." Val tried to get around the crowd in the doorway.

"Let me get you more to drink," Casey said, taking Val's glass from the table. "What did you have?"

"That's okay. I was just—"

"Lemonade," Ryan quickly answered.

"Got it," Casey said and she was gone.

Ryan just shrugged as Val gave him a sharp look bordering on a glare.

"Do you want to play a game?" Robert asked.

"Well, I—"

"We love to play games," Richard added.

"What kind of game are we playing?" Casey asked as she rushed in with Val's refill.

Ryan looked closely at Val. Was it his imagination or was this sharp executive-type lady looking uncomfortable?

"I'm not very good at games."

"Okay," Casey said. "Then we'll play something easy."

"Charades," the boys cried in unison.

Val looked toward Ryan. As he looked in her eyes, all doubt left his mind. The lady was definitely looking for help. He smiled and shrugged.

"Better take your shoes off. These things sometimes take a while."

Val wasn't certain how it happened, but she was assigned to Ryan's team and left alone with him on the porch while Casey took her two brothers into the kitchen to plot their strategy. Through the doorway Val could see the children all huddled together, whispering furiously. Val looked at Ryan.

"I really am no good at games," she told him.

"You said that already." He took a pen from his shirt pocket and reached for the small pieces of paper one of the boys brought over. " 'It doesn't matter who wins or loses, it's how you play the game.' "

"That'll be lousy," she said. "Besides, I was always more a 'Winning isn't everything, it's the only thing' type of person."

"Ah, but just who is winning what?" he said and handed her a piece of paper. "Write down the name of a television show."

Val took the paper, but stared at him. "What kind of television show?"

"Any kind." He wrote down *The Bride of Frankenstein* and folded the paper up tightly. "Your favorite, if you like."

Her favorite? She hardly ever watched television, she preferred books—the longer, the better. She looked over into the kitchen at the kids, busily writing down names and titles that she'd never be able to guess. They were laughing as they wrote, whispering and plotting against Val and their father, but with such childlike innocence that she frowned.

"It's hard to imagine them causing such trouble," she said to Ryan. "They seem like such nice kids."

"They are," he said. "Being nice doesn't preclude being mischievous. You done with that?"

"You two ready yet?" Casey called into the room.

"Not quite," Val answered them both at once and then hurried to write down *The Evening News* on her paper. "It's just that most of the rotten kids I've run across seemed rotten all the time. Yours seem nice."

"Wait until they start winning, then we'll see what you think." Ryan gave her another piece of paper. "How about a famous person?"

He seemed approachable now. The anger that he'd greeted her with had subsided, leaving a gentler, less hostile man. Maybe one who'd be willing to listen to her point of view.

"Most kids who misbehave do so for a reason," she noted as she took the paper from him.

"And I'm the reason for my kids?"

"I didn't say that."

"Didn't you? You said when you came in that you'd give me most of the blame." There was no anger in his voice, no denial, just a weariness that touched her heart, and she wanted to take back her words. "Yes, but I meant—"

"Doesn't matter. I've already blamed myself more than you could ever blame me. It appears that somewhere along the line I did the wrong thing, said the wrong thing. And I continue doing it."

"They just want to be with you," Val said. "Have your undivided attention."

"And when will they not want it? Whenever I say it's time to move on, there's going to be problems. We need someone strong enough to pull us through." He smiled, his eyes lighting up with surprisingly touching warmth. "Hey, maybe you should take the job. The kids like and respect you."

"Only because I'm not their housekeeper," Val pointed out, wanting to avoid those eyes. She stared down at the paper in her hand and scribbled George Washington on it.

"Aren't you done yet?" Casey called once more.

"Yeah, now we are," Ryan said and the kids trooped back in to sit on the sofa across from Val and Ryan.

Val folded up her papers and Ryan put them with his on the coffee table after clearing aside a place in the clutter of magazines, small metal cars and teenage romance books. One of the boys put their pile down separately, then went to sit with Casey and the other twin.

"You can go first," Casey said. "Pick one from our pile."

Ryan glanced at Val, but she just waved her hand toward the pile. She could wait for the chance to make a fool of herself.

"Thanks," Ryan grumbled with good-natured charm and took a folded paper the kids had prepared. They dissolved into giggles at the frown on his face.

"One minute to plan," one of the boys said.

More giggles followed Ryan's deepening scowl but Val hardly noticed as misgivings crowded around her heart. The whole scene was just a bit too cozy for her tastes, too reminiscent of a Norman Rockwell painting of a happy family. Even the knowledge that such things were myths wasn't enough to completely dampen that childlike yearning in her soul to be a real part of things.

It was absolutely crazy, this gentle unfolding of a forgotten flower in her heart. Doubly crazy because she had once had a family. Until her parents had died in that plane crash, she'd been a part of that supposedly magic circle. Except that it had held more bitterness and fights than sweetness and light. After that it had been a series of foster homes, each one teaching better than the last the value of isolating yourself in self-protection.

"All right," Ryan said. "Might as well give this a shot."

"Can I give up now and save time?" she asked.

"Miss Dennison," Casey moaned.

Val smiled and shook her head. "Just joking," she lied.

Ryan got up before her and started moving one hand in a circular motion. What in the world was that?

The dead silence must have gotten to Casey. "It's the name of a movie," the girl told Val.

"Oh. right. I forgot. It's been ages since I played charades."

Ryan held up three fingers and Casey helped out immediately. "Three words."

"Casey," one of the boys protested. "Make her guess herself."

"There's nothing wrong in helping with the rules," she pointed out.

But no amount of rule helping could make Val guess *Pee-Wee's Big Adventure*, and Ryan finally sat down wearily once their time was up.

"Sorry," Val felt bound to say. "But I—"

"I know," he said. "You're not good at games."

"Actually I've never heard of *Pee-Wee's Big Adventure*," she admitted. "I'll do better next time."

Next time came all too quickly after Robert—recognized by Val only because that's what he was called by the others—acted out George Washington to the immediate guessing of the others.

"George Washington?" Ryan repeated with a strange look at her. "You were supposed to pick somebody hard."

"I thought he was hard," she said. "I had no idea how to pantomine 'George'."

"Be a good sport, Daddy," Casey scolded. "It's not Miss Dennison's fault your children are more brilliant than you."

The kids collapsed into a giggling heap, but untangled themselves in time for Casey to give Val some pointers on how to do the book title, *A Tale of Two Cities*. It didn't help. Their time elapsed without Ryan having a clue as to what she was trying to portray. About two seconds later it was Ryan's turn again.

"The others were practice rounds," he announced. "Whoever guesses right in the last round wins."

"No fair."

"That's cheating."

"Hey, they haven't gotten one right yet," Casey told the boys. "We can give them a chance."

The boys groaned and groaned again when Val guessed television show and three words, but they turned to smiles when she was all out of guesses. She had no idea what Ryan was trying to pantomime and knew only a sense of relief when a bell rang in the distance. Surely it was signaling an end to this torture.

"The pizza!" Casey cried and raced toward the front door.

"Oh, boy." The boys followed as Ryan sank onto the wicker love seat next to Val.

"It was 'Felix the Cat'," he told her.

"Who?" She took the paper from him, aware more of the closeness of his thigh to hers, of his arm lying so casually over the back of the small sofa, not near her yet not so very far away either. She forced her eyes to concentrate on the paper in her hand. "Who in the world is Felix the Cat?"

"You've never heard of Felix the Cat?" Ryan's voice was incredulous. "What kind of a childhood did you have? You hardly know the rules to charades and you've never heard of Felix the Cat? Where did you live? In a monastery?"

"Hardly." His eyes were warm, not mocking, but the walls closed in around her heart anyway. Her life, her childhood, was not open to discussion. Not now, not ever. She'd learned to bury the past long ago and had yet to find a reason to unearth it. She got to her feet and found her purse on the floor nearby. "I'd really better be going. I've stayed longer than I intended as it is."

Casey had just come in the door, a steaming pizza box in her arms. "Aren't you staying for dinner?" she asked.

"But we never finished our game," Robert pointed out.

"You guys won," she said even as she slid around past them, steeling herself against the disappointment in their eyes and their voices. When Val turned to say goodbye to Ryan though, she found he was right behind her.

"Well, you'll be hearing from me early next week with another prospect."

"Okay." His eyes seemed to be saying more than his words were, but she didn't let his gaze hold hers long enough for him to read her soul, assuming there was anything visible for him to read. "I'll be waiting for your call."

"Right." She wasn't fleeing, she told herself as she hurried through the house to the front door, but still sighed in relief when she was out in her minivan and away from those probing eyes. A housekeeper, that's what she'd get them. Then she'd be through with all these childish games. She didn't bother to ask her heart just which games she was referring to.

Another name rolled up onto the video display screen Monday morning and the computer beeped as if asking if that person was satisfactory. It seemed to Val that she'd already looked at a thousand names as she slapped the "next record" key with a special vigor.

"I take it that's another no."

Val glanced across the desk to where Ryan Crawford sat, one leg crossed over the other at the knee, his arms resting in relaxed repose in his lap. His ease annoyed her. "I told you I'd call when I had a suitable candidate," she pointed out.

"No problem. I was just in the area and thought I'd drop by."

"I thought you had a business that was demanding more and more of your time," she pointed out as she slapped at the key to bring up yet another candidate for Ryan Crawford's housekeeper.

"You have to spend money to make money. I have to give up some time in order to free up more time."

Whack—another candidate popped up. "I wasn't going to forget about you," Val grumbled.

"Never thought you would."

She hadn't forgotten much about Friday evening at his house either. Not the way his kids accepted her into their family, not the way her heart stirred at his nearness, and not the way his eyes tried to probe into her soul. Every one a valid reason to find him a housekeeper as soon as possible. Val glanced over and met Ryan's eyes. They were assessing, not pressing, their darkness more gentle and kind than demanding. Val got up suddenly and marched into her secretary's office.

"Do you know who Felix the Cat is?" Val asked.

There was a long silence as Marcie stared at her. The woman was probably surprised at the question, but she was no more surprised than Val, who found it hard to believe that her mouth had uttered those words.

"Yeah," Marcie finally responded, releasing each word slowly and carefully. "He's a black cartoon cat. His cartoons were on TV a lot about fifteen to twenty years ago. Why are you asking?"

"I was just curious," Val said and went back to her desk.

Whack. Val sent another candidate to the oblivion of electronic bits and solid circuits. Was she going to have to check out the whole country to find the Crawfords a housekeeper?

"How do you decide which housekeepers to reject?" Ryan asked.

She glanced up at him, but only for a split second as if the screen before her was too fascinating to be distracted from. "Some of them only want part-time work, some don't want to live in, some don't want childcare responsibilities. There are all sorts of reasons."

"Oh."

Whack. Damn. Why didn't the man stop watching her? She had a good reason not to know who that stupid cat was. It wasn't as if he was someone famous, like the Cheshire cat in *Alice in Wonderland*.

Her eyes blurred and Val had to blink a few times to focus on the next candidate that came dancing onto the screen. After her parents had died she'd become emotionally independent. Too old to have any real chance for adoption, she had made the rounds of foster homes, staying for as little as a few days in some, as long as six months in others. She had learned quickly not to care for anything or anyone, because everything was temporary and totally out of her control. The system could snatch her out of one home and place her in another without warning, usually for reasons that had nothing to do with her.

Whack. Her keystroking was getting too robust and she took a couple of deep breaths to reassert her self-control. She didn't need a broken keyboard just because Ryan Crawford had awoken unwanted memories.

That stupid cat was a television character and she had rarely watched television. The sets were always in living rooms, places for gathering, and she had known that if she gathered she would get close. And the closer one became, the more it hurt to separate.

So her escape had been books, books of all kinds, but especially beautiful novels filled with good, caring people and happy endings. Books had been better than TV because they were portable. They were friends who would go anywhere she went. She could visit with them at the library, on a park bench, or in a solitary corner in whatever house she was staying in. Reading had not only given her friends, it had also enhanced her academic talents. In spite of numerous transfers, she'd always gotten good grades in school; then she'd received a small college scholarship and entrance to a work-study program. College had brought more books and an end to foster homes, but no more friends. After all those years of locking people out, she hadn't known how to open herself up to let anyone in.

Then Danny had walked into her life. At first she hadn't known what he saw in her. He was tall, startlingly handsome and the quarterback on the football team. He could have had any girl on campus, but finally she'd quit questioning his choice of her and accepted him. She opened herself up to him totally, and when her roommate moved out, Danny moved in. They were ecstatically happy until an intruder barged into their lives, or at least that's what Danny had called the baby. He'd wanted her to have an abortion, but she couldn't. It was a living thing, this tiny flower of her and Danny's love. She was sure that with time Danny would learn to love the baby as she already did, but he never even tried. He left and found another girlfriend quick enough, another mouse like herself, willing to give him anything and everything. Val was alone, with nothing.

Actually it wasn't nothing and she certainly wasn't alone. She was left with a growing stomach, a sore back, swelling ankles and a little being who kicked her ribs all night. Soon she didn't have the strength for school *and* work. If she gave up her job she'd have no way to live, so she dropped out of her classes and worked as close up to her delivery as possible. By the time her son kicked his way out into the world, she was totally drained. There had been nothing left in her to give, no energy, no strength, no emotions. Absolutely nothing. After several counseling sessions, Val knew it was better to let a family have him, one that could provide the kind of life she couldn't. A family who knew how to love and be loved.

No tears came anymore—Val had shed them long ago. Even this rare skipping down memory lane wasn't about to bring them back. That was all in the past and what was done was done. Life wasn't a game where you could declare a forfeit and reschedule with the hope that it would go better later. All she hoped for now was the day she'd find her son again, see him and know that he was well and happy.

"That a possibility?" Ryan asked.

Val forced her eyes to focus on the screen she'd been staring at, trying to make sense of his words. Housekeepers, that was why he was here. And as a matter of fact, this woman was a possibility, a definite possibility. "I think this woman may just be what you're looking for," Val said. "She'll provide the discipline that your children need."

She heard Ryan's footsteps on the rug as he came up directly behind her. "Alecia Huntsen," Ryan read off the screen.

Privately known around the office as Alecia the Hun, but Val pushed that thought away. Alecia wasn't mean, just firm. "I'll call her this afternoon and see when she can start," Val said definitely, so that her conscience would think twice before questioning her decision.

"Great. You'll call me at my office to let me know?"

"I will," Val agreed, walking briskly with him toward the door.

Alecia was agreeable to starting Wednesday and, wonder of wonders, didn't call to resign by noon. Val resisted the temptation to call the Crawford household and find out if the boys had cut the phone lines. By Thursday she was smiling in happy assurance that she'd found someone strong enough to take on the twins, and by Friday she was even chuckling about the game of charades. So when the phone rang early Saturday afternoon in the midst of Val's own housecleaning, the Crawfords were the last thing on her mind.

"Miss Dennison? This is Casey Crawford." Casey, speaking with a weak, pale imitation of her normally bubbly voice, said, "I'm afraid Mrs. Huntsen just isn't working out."

"Oh?"

Val's single word apparently spoke volumes to Casey, for she immediately sprang to a defense. "It has nothing to do with us messing up," she said. "Daddy had a real long talk with us before she came and we saw how important his business is to him and how he didn't need us acting like spoiled brats."

Casey paused and Val could only swallow the lump that had appeared in her throat. She knew that Ryan had made sacrifices after his wife had died, but one didn't stop being a parent after a year or two. When you signed up, you signed up for the duration or not at all. Why couldn't he see that his kids were afraid of losing *him* too?

"We tried hard, Miss Dennison, real hard," Casey said. "It's just not working."

Val clenched her jaws for a moment. What could she do? The kids needed a housekeeper who could control them, for their safety if not for their happiness. She should just tell Casey to hang in there, to try to please Alecia and things would get better.

"You have—"

But Casey went on as if Val hadn't spoken. "Mrs. Huntsen is a real neat freak. I'm pretty neat with my room and stuff, so she doesn't bother me, but she really rides the boys hard."

"I take it your brothers are not neat freaks."

Casey managed to cough up a short laugh. "Not really. They're a lot like Dad."

"So it's inherited," Val said.

"Yeah. I guess they're pretty much superslobs," Casey said. "They are trying but it seems like she's always punishing them for something. I mean it seems that they get yelled at if they have a sock crooked in their drawer."

Val sighed. Alecia Huntsen had a reputation as a disciplinarian. Was she being too tough? It could very well have happened, especially after getting a speech from Val and then from Ryan Crawford about how desperately his children needed a firm hand.

Maybe the kids were changing and Alecia just came in at the wrong time with the wrong methods. Or, Casey could be giving Val another one of her con jobs. Val sighed. She should just give old Ryan a call and tell him to straighten out his family. This wasn't her affair.

"Isn't your father there?" Val finally asked. "Have you talked to him about it?"

"He's working today," Casey said. "You know, to catch up after all the time he's missed lately."

Swell.

"I don't know what to do, Miss Dennison," Casey repeated. "Richard's been in his room crying all afternoon and he won't even tell me why."

So they were being hoist by their own petard, stewing in their own juices, reaping what they had sown. It served them right. "I'll be over and have a chat with everyone," Val said with a sigh.

"Well, if you don't have other more important things to do," Casey said, suddenly seeming reluctant to impose.

"Anything else to do?" Val laughed. "It's Saturday, Casey. I don't work on weekends. I'm just sitting around eating bonbons."

"Oh, good," Casey replied. "It's okay then."

As Val hung up, a heavy weariness settled on her shoulders. Sarcasm was wasted on the young.

She checked herself in the mirror. Her short hair was held back by a sweatband. A T-shirt, shorts, and old sandals completed her outfit. She probably should dress a little more suitably for a customer visit, but the hell with it. This wasn't her fault or her idea. Besides, Mr. Ryan Crawford was hiding out in his precious office, so who would know?

Chapter Three

The screeching tires of Ryan's own car echoed in his ears. His heart leapt into his mouth as he practically stood his car on its nose. His front fender stopped just inches from the bumper ahead of him, and Ryan's heart slowly sank back into his chest.

Damn! His Ford and that Pontiac up ahead had almost become one. Just a few split seconds of inattention and he'd nearly caused an accident. In reality, it probably wouldn't have been that serious. They were traveling in downtown Fort Wayne and traffic was going barely twenty-five miles an hour. But what would have happened if he'd been distracted on an expressway or a country road?

A horn sounded behind him and Ryan waved cheerfully, setting his car in motion once more. His eyes carefully scanned the scene before him as well as the rearview mirror as he fought to keep his attention on the road but, like a team of commandos sneaking onto an enemy beach, his worries moved back into his consciousness. He shook his head and sighed.

At least this housekeeper issue was finally settled, he reminded himself. He no longer had to worry about leaving the kids each day, wondering when their mischief would backfire and one of them would get hurt. No, Home Services, Incorporated had come through. This new housekeeper seemed more than competent, she seemed a battle-hardened veteran. Just what they needed.

Oh? his heart questioned, mocking the certainty his thoughts wanted to convey. If he was so pleased with the battle-ax, why then did he rush out of the house earlier and earlier each morning to avoid seeing the pleading in the kids' eyes? Why did he have to gird himself to be cheerful and smiling when he went into the house each evening to balance out the gloom in the air? Why had he invited everyone he'd been working with this afternoon on that Kidney Foundation project over to the house tonight for dinner instead of going out with them someplace closer to the office?

Because he knew the kids weren't happy, that's why.

But what was the alternative? Stay at home forever and never be able to save enough for their college educations? Swallow his own ambitions and need for adult companionship until the kids were grown? If he let them win this battle, would they ever be willing to let go of him, or would he be making them emotionally dependent on him forever?

He slowed his car and turned a corner. Maybe he ought to marry again, give the kids a semblance of normality in their lives. But he vetoed that idea almost as quickly as he thought it. Marrying for the kids' sake was only another in a long line of lousy ideas he'd had lately. Hell, if he couldn't find the right housekeeper, how did he think he could find the right wife? Besides, sharing his life, and the kids' lives with someone was the last thing he wanted. The very idea of it hurt, like bumping a bruise you'd thought had healed.

He pulled his car into the driveway, stopping behind a pale blue minivan. Whose was it? The office crowd had planned to work another hour before coming out here. Had someone changed his mind and beaten Ryan home?

Ryan climbed out the car door slowly. The minivan ahead of him looked familiar. Had he seen it before or was it just another of the thousands of blue minivans that seemed to be swarming over the roads these days?

The door opened as he hurried up the sidewalk and Mrs. Huntsen came out, carrying two suitcases and a swaying rubber tree plant whose leaves tried unsuccessfully to block her frown. He stopped in astonishment.

"You may take me to my apartment," she told him, marching past him toward the car. "I shall not stay where I'm not wanted."

Ryan's heart sank into an all-too-familiar gloom as he glanced fleetingly at the door. Two solemn little faces peered out, but Ryan turned away, starting after the housekeeper. Time enough to learn of the twins' mischief later.

"Not wanted?" he asked Mrs. Huntsen, burying deep all his earlier misgivings. "How can you say that? I've been very happy with your work. And if the kids—"

She'd stopped at the back of the car, dropping the bags as she waited for him to open the trunk. "Not the children, Mr. Crawford. I can handle any child alive. It was her—Ms. Dennison—who told me to go."

She nodded toward the door where his startled eyes found Val Dennison standing. The twins were on either side of her, and Casey was watching the whole thing by peeking around Val's shoulder. Now what havoc had that woman wreaked in their lives?

He remembered with sudden clarity the calm, the serenity that Val had brought with her last week when she'd come to the house. And how he'd wanted to keep her there for a while to hold back the chaos that always seemed ready to swallow them up. He—Ryan Michael Crawford—had wanted to cling to her as the kids wanted to cling to him. The memory both frightened and irritated him. The irritation won out and Mrs. Huntsen became the battleground. Keep her here and it would keep Val away.

Ryan opened the front door of his car, but made no move to put Mrs. Huntsen's luggage inside the trunk. "Look, I'm certain there's been a misunderstanding," he told the woman. "Why don't you sit down and I'll try to straighten this all out?"

"There's nothing to straighten out," the woman insisted, getting into the car. Her eyes stared straight ahead, her jaw was locked tight.

Ryan said nothing, just turned and strode back up the walk of the old, three-story gingerbread Victorian. "Hi, Dad," all the kids chorused.

"Hi," he said as he nodded at them, but his eyes met Val's. "What happened with Mrs. Huntsen?"

"I suggested she might be happier elsewhere."

"You suggested? What right did you have to suggest anything if we were happy with her?" Ryan asked, rudely pushing out of his mind the doubts that had plagued him as he drove home.

"She threw away Mikey," Val shot right back at him.

Ryan bit back a sigh. Mikey was a decrepit, old stuffed dog that Richard had resurrected from the attic to sleep with after Maggie had died. Ryan looked down at the boy, who held the dog tightly in one arm.

"I'm sure it was an accident," Ryan said. "The important thing is that you got him back."

Richard said nothing. He just moved a step closer to Val. Ryan realized that the boy was clinging to her hand and for some reason that annoyed him more than anything. He was feeling suffocated by the kids' clinging at times, but he didn't want them clinging to anyone else, especially not this woman with the distant eyes. Especially not to the woman he'd wanted to cling to last week.

"She just didn't know how important he was to you," Ryan told Richard.

"That doesn't matter," Val said, ignoring the fact that he'd been talking to the boy. "She had no right to throw anything of Richard's away."

"I am paying her to keep the place clean, you know."

"But not to throw out things that are valuable."

"The toy is bald and filthy. How was Mrs. Huntsen to know it meant something?"

"Meaningful or meaningless isn't the issue," Val snapped. "It's control. Richard has the right to decide which of his possessions he keeps and which are disposed of."

He knew she was right, but still anger, exhaustion and a sense of defeat all combined to drain his energy, twist his stomach, and tie his brain into knots. "It's not enough of a reason to fire her," he said lamely.

"I didn't fire her. I'll place her somewhere else and find you another housekeeper. Unless you'd rather work with another agency; then I'll refund the money you've paid."

She had an answer for everything and his temper exploded. "I don't care about the damn money," he snapped, knowing as the words passed his lips that he shouldn't be saying what he was, but he'd had it with just about everything. With his chaos and her calm, with his taking a battle-ax's side against his son, with trying to be everything to his children and failing miserably. "Keep the money. Use it for a vacation. Give it to your favorite charity. I don't care."

Ryan's torrent of words exhausted him and the shocked look on his children's faces brought a load of guilt upon his shoulders. Now he was even more tired than before. He ran his fingers through his hair as if he could set his ill humor free that way.

"I'm sorry," he said quietly.

But she didn't look angry and the lines of irritability were fading from her face as something else warmed her eyes. The anger started to build in him again and he wanted to scream that he didn't need anybody's pity, but he held back. The kids were still there, still staring wide-eyed.

"Look, this whole thing has thrown me. I didn't mean to blow up like that. I'll just take Mrs. Huntsen home." He paused, taking in Val's casual attire: her long legs, muscled and lightly tanned, the T-shirt that strained across her breasts, and her short curly hair that in its very disarray seemed to invite touching and further mussing. He suppressed long-dormant feelings of lust and forced a smile to his face. "Now why don't you go home and continue your well-earned weekend of relaxation?"

"If you want, I'll stay here with the kids until you return," she offered.

It was her voice that pushed back the chaos. Her eyes were cool and distant, gray with ice chips that held no invitation, but her voice was husky and warm. Her words were delivered slowly with just a hint of a Texas drawl; molasses sliding down his overwrought nerves. Tension didn't stand a chance. He knew enough to be wary.

"No, that's all right." The kids were all he wanted to come home to. "The kids will be fine. Casey can manage."

He started to turn away, when another cloud came to join the crowd hanging over his head. "Oh Lord, I almost forgot. I told everybody from the office to come here after work for some supper. I'll have to stop at the Chicken Coop and pick up a couple of buckets of fried chicken on my way back, so I'll be a bit longer."

"You invited guests here tonight?" Val asked. Her frown held only concern, not censure. "Mrs. Huntsen didn't say anything about guests."

Something about her tone though set his defenses in place once more. "It's not a big deal. I'm just going to get some fried chicken, pop and beer, and a bag or two of potato chips. I didn't promise anybody a sit-down, gourmet meal."

Her eyes narrowed into cold, gray slits. "How many people?"

Ryan shrugged. "Fifteen, maybe twenty." He shrugged again. "There were some people who work for me, some for the Kidney Foundation and then a few spouses and dates."

"You've got twenty people coming for dinner and I discharge your housekeeper." She sighed. "No wonder you blew up. I'll stay and help."

"That won't be necessary. Thanks anyway."

"We can help," Casey added.

He smiled at her. "Right, kiddo. It won't be hard."

Val did not look convinced. "What about glasses and plates? Do you have enough tableware for twenty people? How about napkins, chairs, ice?"

He could feel his temper rising again with each question she asked, with each question that he couldn't answer. "We'll manage," he said tersely.

"Are these all employees of yours?" she asked. "Or are they customers?"

Casey seemed to catch some of the worry Val was sprinkling liberally through the air. "They're customers," she told Val. "Or Daddy hopes they'll be. That's what they've been working on the past week—a presentation of all the ideas they have for helping the Kidney Foundation raise money, especially to help sick kids."

Ryan watched his daughter with both pride and exasperation. He was proud that she was aware of what he was doing, that she cared enough to remember what he said over the dinner table, but exasperated that she was giving Val further ammunition.

"So a lot's riding on this dinner," Val said.

"They'll judge me on my work, not my dinner," he argued.

"Competency is competency," she pronounced. "You may have it in your work, but I haven't seen much of it around here. I'm staying."

"Fine," he snapped, giving in though his pride refused to let it be a gracious defeat. "Stay then. I guess beggars can't be choosers."

"Mr. Crawford," Val said slowly. "Why don't you take your overpowering charm and drive Mrs. Huntsen home?"

"That sounds like a good idea," he replied. "This area is already knee-deep in warmth and friendliness."

Val flashed him a hard smile as she turned around. "Skip the Chicken Coop though. I'll handle the edibles."

"Bye, Daddy," his kids chorused as they followed Miss Warmth into the house.

Ryan shook his head as he made his way back to his car. She was tough, quick and competent, but it would take someone feeling exceptionally brave and foolish to see if there was a heart buried under all that capability. At the moment he was feeling neither.

Val marched the kids through the kitchen and onto the porch, her eyes finding the traffic patterns and conversation pits where guests would end up. She sighed. The house was clean. Alecia must have worked overtime to remove all the clutter, but it wasn't really set up for a party. It would have to do though, since Val had less than an hour to get everything ready.

"All right now. Robert, you clear off that buffet table. Put the flowers in the living room, the magazines on the bookshelf and the Legos away." When one little boy trudged off, she turned to the other, still holding his stuffed dog though not with the same fervor. "Richard, find some tablecloths for me and an ice bucket. Casey, get out the glassware, but stick to the plain stuff. Nothing with Mickey Mouse, or Purdue University or Colts emblems on them.''

The kids were surprisingly cooperative, all scurrying off to their appointed tasks, leaving Val free to make some calls. Fifteen minutes later, the beer, wine, ice and assorted sodas were on their way. Ten minutes after that, the food was ordered along with plates, napkins and tableware. That left her with appetizers to prepare and the nagging question of why she was doing this.

The appetizers were easier than finding the reason for her motives. Ryan had a good selection of fresh vegetables in the refrigerator that would do quite well sliced up and served with some buttermilk salad dressing. Once her hands were involved in cutting the carrots up into sticks, her mind began to meander back to the question of motives.

Why was she doing all this? All right, she'd discharged his housekeeper without asking about his plans, but he could have managed with Chicken Coop fried chicken and potato chips. Why did she feel the need to ride to his rescue like some Joan of Arc?

She finished up the carrots and started on the celery, but the stalks held no more answers than the carrots had. Maybe it was the kids that left her feeling vulnerable, left her wanting to play superwoman. No, the kids were why she came, not why she stayed.

She stayed because of something perverse inside her, something that needed to prove that this house, this family, couldn't touch her. She could stay here and organize their dinner party on the spur of the moment, and with an hour's notice she could put together an evening that would run as smoothly as if it had been in planning for weeks—but she wouldn't fall back once to her childish dreams.

Ryan returned soon after she'd started on the green peppers, while Casey and the boys were setting up a makeshift bar on the buffet. He'd taken his suit coat off along with his tie, loosening the collar of his shirt somewhere along the way too. His hair was mussed in a way that was becoming all too familiar to her. She concentrated on the green pepper she was slicing.

"Hope you didn't have great plans for all these vegetables," she said.

"Just to fill my kids with vitamins."

"So your guests will get them instead." She chanced a glance up at him. His eyes were smiling, dark pools that were as warm and welcoming as hot coffee in the morning. She went back to her green pepper slicing.

"What can I do?" he asked.

She nodded toward the pile of sliced vegetables. "Find a tray or plate and arrange them into some sort of order. A bowl of buttermilk salad dressing should go in the middle as a dip."

"Aye, aye, captain." He brought a silver tray over and put a small glass bowl of the dressing in the middle, then began to arrange the vegetables around it. "This doesn't look too neat."

"It doesn't have to look perfect, just edible." She sneaked another glance at him and caught his frown of concentration, then her eyes went to the tray. It looked remarkably like him and his house, in pre-Alecia days. Ordered disarray. She couldn't help but laugh.

"I told you they weren't behaving," he said.

But she just shook her head. "It looks fine. I've learned not to trust anything that looks perfect."

"Oh?"

She thought briefly of Danny with his perfect good looks and football physique, but banished him back to the past with a shake of her head. "I had a neighbor when I was a kid who could bake the most beautiful pies," she said. "Every crimp around the edges was exact, the crust was always golden brown and they smelled good enough to die for."

"But they were filled with ground glass?"

"Not quite, but they tasted awful. She just couldn't get the knack of making fillings. Her pies always sold well at the church bazaars though."

"But not many repeat buyers, I bet."

"Enough." Val finished the last of the green peppers and washed the paring knife. "You'd be surprised how many people forget or decide the fault had to lie with them since the pies looked so perfect."

Hadn't she felt that way for a time after Danny left? But she was strong, stronger than most, and knew that the flaws in Danny's perfection weren't due to her.

"Guess I'm guilty of that too," Ryan said suddenly, a sheepish grin warming his voice but setting her nerves on edge.

"Oh?" He was too comfortable to be around. He acted as if they were old friends, not mere acquaintances, and her silly heart was accepting that as fact. She worked on rinsing the seeds and peels down the garbage disposal.

"I knew things weren't going well around here," he told her. "But I tried to accept the appearance of perfection rather than ask questions. I guess the kids aren't the only ones having trouble adjusting to my new work habits. Sorry I took my frustrations out on you."

"That's okay," she said as she looked around the kitchen. She didn't think there was anything left to be done.

"Val, somebody's here with the drinks," Casey called from the other room.

"Send them in here," Val called back and for the next few minutes was involved with setting up the bar. By the time that was done, she was back in control. Ryan's half smile as he watched her had no effect.

"Must be nice to have connections," he said.

"Home Services, Incorporated offers a complete line of... home services." She straightened a wineglass that was slightly out of line with the others.

"Oh, does it?"

His words were innocent, but his tone mocked, setting a blush to her cheeks. She glanced at her watch rather than at him. "The food should be here anytime now. I was lucky. The caterer I called had overcooked for a wedding this afternoon so I was able to get lasagna, tossed salad and Italian bread rather than just cold cuts or Swedish meatballs. Once he gets here, I'll be on my way."

He frowned. Her eyes had mistakenly glanced his way and were caught. "Can't you stay and enjoy the fruits of your labors?" he asked; then his frown deepened. "What am I saying? It's a Saturday night. You must have plans already."

Of course she had, the same plans she had for every Saturday night: go down to the health club, play a few sets of Saturday singles tennis round-robin, then join the others at the Purple Ox for a few drinks. It wasn't terribly exciting. It wasn't even mildly exciting. But it was her chosen ritual, her time each week to mingle socially, and the constantly shifting sands of attendees suited her preferences.

"It's not just that I had plans," she told him. "I'm hardly dressed for your get-together."

His eyes followed her hands as they waved down at her shorts and T-shirt, but rather than agree, he just deepened his grin. "Oh, I rather like the way you're dressed, but if that's all that's stopping you, borrow something from Casey. You're almost the same size."

"Casey's a good four inches shorter than I am," Val pointed out.

He shrugged. "Aren't miniskirts coming back into style?"

"Not that mini."

"She's got to have something," he said and went to the door. "Casey, what clothes have you got that would fit Miss Dennison?"

Before Val could protest that she didn't want to stay anyway, Casey was in the kitchen. "You're staying for the party? Oh, wow. Terrific even. Want to wear my red skirt? That would look dreamy on you. Much better than it does on me."

The twins were somehow there also. "You're staying for the party?" Robert grumbled.

So she wasn't as popular as she thought, Val told herself with an inexplicable sinking of her stomach.

"You'd have more fun upstairs. Watching a videotape with me and Robert," Richard said. "Dad got us *Tarzan Meets Godzilla* to watch after the ball game."

Val burst out laughing, at herself as well as at the movie title. "I think I can pass on that one. I'm not staying to have a good time but to make sure the party runs smoothly. It's part of my job."

And that was the only reason, she told herself more sternly as Casey led her off to her bedroom.

An hour later Val was overseeing dinner as Ryan's guests wove through the buffet line. Casey's skirt was ankle length on the girl but calf length on Val. This combined with a loose-fitting cotton sweater, she was dressed slightly less formally than the others, but not much so. She felt at ease, enjoying herself as she refilled dishes and kept the bar supplied with clean glasses.

"This isn't as much fun as I thought it would be," Casey confided as they carried dirty glasses to the kitchen.

"What did you expect?" Val asked. "Surely not anyone your own age."

"I don't know." Casey shrugged as she put the glasses on the counter. "All anybody's talking about is business."

"What else would they be doing?" Val asked with a laugh. "Playing charades?"

Casey just sighed and began to load the glasses into the dishwasher. "It used to be different," she said. "Before Mom died, their parties would be lots of fun. Everybody laughing all the time."

Val grabbed another tray of clean glasses and shook her head. "This isn't a real party, you know," she pointed out. "It's an extension of their meetings all day. Maybe you're trying to make it into something it isn't."

She pushed through the swinging kitchen door and out into the dining room. A small group of people were at the buffet taking seconds.

"Can you believe the way the Cubs played in that last home series?" one man asked another.

"Maybe this'll be their year."

"Who're you kidding? They'll fold like they do every year."

So not *everybody* was talking about business, Val noted, despite what Casey thought. She put the clean glasses down and went around gathering up dirty plates.

The guests gathered around the bar were talking movies. Those on the porch were into vacation plans. Only the group in the living room was talking business and that discussion seemed led by Ryan.

"Ads are effective, all right, but how much real money do they generate?" he was asking. "You've got to make each person feel that his contribution is needed."

"But we're aiming for awareness too. Where does the focus need to be?"

Val picked up two empty plates from an end table and brought them all back to the kitchen. Casey was fixing a tray of pastries for dessert.

"Well, is it as boring as I said? Or worse?" she asked.

"Actually there are lots of different conversations going on," Val said. "It's only normal that your father be preoccupied with business since he's running this show. Why don't we take the tray from group to group rather than leaving it on the buffet?"

While Casey took the tray, Val carried small plates and clean forks around. The dining room group had switched to arguing over the reality of psychic phenomena, the porch group was discussing the relative merits of golf courses around the midwest, but the group in the living room was still on business.

"Everybody's targeting that group. What do the demographics say?" Ryan asked.

Casey raised her eyebrows at Val as her father waved aside the dessert tray. He seemed excited about what he was saying, yet Val sensed something else under the surface, a tension almost that was driving him. The evening seemed to be running smoothly, so what was making him tense?

She ignored her rule of noninvolvement when she and Casey got back to the kitchen. "I thought you said your father was dating again. Did he cancel plans of his own for this evening?" Val asked as she refilled the pastry tray.

Casey laughed. "His dates haven't been too frequent or too successful and I think he got pushed into most of them. You know, somebody from work has a cousin visiting from out of town."

"So they were more business than anything else," Val noted. "I thought you were worried he was going to get married again."

"We are, because he *doesn't* date anyone he cares about. Sometimes he seems to be thinking that marriage would solve all our problems. But he'd just choose someone who seemed competent, not someone any of us cared for."

The girl's bright blue eyes were shadowed with worry, but Val had to smile. "I think your're getting upset over nothing," Val assured her, picking up the tray. "Your father's an adult. He's not going to rush into anything for the wrong reasons. Trust his judgment."

Casey seemed to relax slightly and she gave Val a lopsided grin. "I guess you're right."

"I know I am." Val pushed open the kitchen door with her back and carried the tray back through the dining room toward the buffet. As she passed the door, she glanced into the living room where Ryan was still engrossed in talking business. His smile seemed genuine but there was something strangely familiar about the way he held his head.

It reminded her of Richard that afternoon when she had come here to discover that Alecia had thrown out his precious stuffed dog. There had been something lost about Richard then, a sort of worried fear that she thought she saw in Ryan for just a split second.

Maybe she was wrong, yet a smidgen of doubt remained. Was Ryan likely to do something foolish in his desire to find security again?

Chapter Four

Come on, Miss Dennison, stay just a few minutes," Robert begged. "It's not really that scary."

"Anything that features a monster eating buildings is scary." Val set down the plate of desserts on the coffee table. "Hope you guys like chocolate, or is that like asking if Godzilla likes skyscrapers?"

"Chocolate's great," Richard assured her as both boys reached for their pieces of cake.

The den was quiet except for the sound of munching—cake and buildings. Only vague noises from downstairs were floating up. Val felt tired all of a sudden. The sofa seemed to beckon enticingly and she had the urge to curl up there. It was time to get home.

"We've been really good, haven't we?" one of the boys asked.

Val turned, realizing that they'd been talking to her, but she'd missed the beginning of what they'd said. "I'm sorry, boys. What did you say?"

"We said, we've been really good," Richard said.

"We really have," Robert added.

"But we'd like some company, too."

"Can't you stay and watch the movie with us?"

"We'll tell you when a scary part is coming so you can close your eyes."

They were such con artists! She wondered what devilment they had in mind, though she decided that maybe they were just lonely. And they had been good. Suddenly it wasn't just the idea of relaxing in the peace and quiet up here that was so inviting, but the relaxing up here with the boys. Watching a ridiculous movie and listening to their silly jokes seemed infinitely more appealing than hurrying off to her empty home.

"All right," she said. "After I clean things up a bit downstairs, I'll come up and watch Godzilla with you, but not the whole movie. I have to get home."

"It's only ten o'clock."

"And past my bedtime," Val assured them as she went out the door. "I'll be back soon."

What cleaning up there was to do shouldn't take long, Val thought as she went back down the hall, past Casey's room. Val had insisted she take a break, and now the girl was sequestered with her phone. Val continued on, past the boys' room and past what must be Ryan's room. She was slightly tempted to look inside, to see what kind of a man he was under all his businesslike demeanor, but she kept her feet moving.

There was no reason for her to want to know any more about Ryan—except for idle curiosity. She wasn't about to give in to that so she hurried through the downstairs room with the dwindling clusters of guests and into the kitchen. She had just filled the sink with hot, soapy water when Ryan came in.

"Everything was perfect," he said. "I can't thank you enough for helping out."

Ryan caught her unawares and vulnerable. His tall body seemed to fill up the room. His presence would have been almost intimidating, except that his mussed hair and boyish grin tried to convince her he was harmless. But she knew harmless wasn't the word to describe this man.

"It was nothing," she said, to herself as much as to him, as she turned back to the sink.

"Hey, you don't have to do all that," he protested. "I'll clean up tomorrow. You've done enough as it is."

"It's all right. There's not much to do. Casey already washed a bunch of stuff that was too big to go in the dishwasher. I'm just going to finish up this bunch. Then I'll watch T.V. with the boys."

He took a step closer. She could feel it even though her back was to him.

"I don't like the idea of your driving home by yourself," he said. "Ted and I are going to redo a few things in our presentation once everyone has gone, but that should take only a half hour or so. I'll drive you home after that."

"That's silly," she said, and put the crystal salad bowl into the dish drainer. "I've driven by myself at night before."

Ryan picked up a towel, then the salad bowl, and began to dry it. "No, I'm responsible for you being out this late. I'll drive you."

"That would leave my car here," she pointed out.

"I'll drive your car."

She cleared her throat, getting her walls of control back in place as she washed the salad fork and spoon, then turned to face him. "That would still leave my car here when you drove yourself home."

"Then I'll follow you home," he said. His hand brushed hers as he reached for the salad utensils. A wave of longing coursed over her, warmth washing over loneliness, wistfulness being drowned by a sense of belonging. None of which she greeted with enthusiasm.

Val grabbed the spatula used to serve the lasagna and concentrated on scrubbing off all the dried pasta. She shouldn't have let her hands linger over those utensils so, not if she hadn't wanted him to touch her. She wasn't a love-starved female; she dated fairly often. All right, not anyone special, but that was by her choice. There were any number of men she could be having a serious relationship with if she wanted.

Why then had her heart leapt when Ryan came in the room? Why did his touch set it smiling? Because she was tired, she told herself. She had had a long week and needed a good night's sleep.

She put the cleaned spatula into the sink while he was putting the salad utensils away. Not because she was afraid to risk his touch again, but because she was sure she'd gotten every last speck of sauce off it.

"Tell me, do your clients usually take up so much of your time?" Ryan asked. "Or are we more trouble than most?"

"Oh, each case is unique," she said vaguely and washed several knives.

"Meaning we're more trouble than most," he said. His voice softened her resolve and she couldn't help but smile.

"It was my own fault," she pointed out. "I was the one who discharged Mrs. Huntsen. I don't know what she had planned, but she certainly wouldn't have needed my help."

He grinned. He looked just like the twins did when they were about to be caught in some mischief. "Actually she didn't know about the people I'd invited. It was sort of a spur-of-the-moment decision."

Val stopped washing to stare at him. "You mean you were just going to spring it on her when you got home?"

"I had it planned out though. Chicken Coop fried chicken, potato chips, soda, beer and wine. What was there for her to do?"

"What was there for her to do?" Val repeated, then burst into laughter, leaning against the counter for support. "Boy, are you lucky I got here before you did. Alecia would have skinned you alive. She's not a lady who likes surprises."

"Hey, I had everything covered." His eyes were alight with humor.

"Except for the disruption of her routine, the getting ready and the cleaning up and the selection of a menu that would do anyone involved credit," Val pointed out the best she could between her laughter.

"So I missed a few things."

"Just a few."

"I guess I'm lucky I had you around," he said, and everything changed.

Val's laughter had worn down the walls she lived behind and awakened her hungers that she thought she'd outgrown. The need to have someone to share laughter and tears with, to have people who cared when she was tired, to have a place where she belonged. The feelings came over her so strongly, so unexpectedly, that she couldn't speak.

Ryan reached over and kissed her lips gently, spreading warmth into all the corners of her soul. It was as if spring had come, melting the winter snows in one blinding moment to leave a blanket of sunshine and flowers over her.

He took her hand as he pulled back. "I guess I'd better get back to my guests, but remember I'm going to see you home. No arguments, either. I take my responsibilities seriously."

His warm hand was holding her lightly but somehow it kept her from pulling free. Part of her liked the feel of his skin against hers, but part of her cried out against the closeness. The numbing shock that first accompanied his kiss was wearing off; her mind was crying out against her sudden weakness. This was all part of what she'd had long ago and what she no longer wanted. With strength mined from some forgotten source, she turned her gaze back to the sink, and once her eyes were free of his, her hand was free also.

"Let's just see how much more work you still have to do when I'm ready to leave," she said easily as she submerged the appetizer tray.

"No sneaking out behind my back," he said.

Reaching around her, he sneaked a crumb of chocolate cake off the pastry tray, his arm brushing hers in the process. A shiver raced along her spine, her heart speeding up at the gentle contact and hungering for more.

"No," she almost snapped, then took a steadying breath. "No, no sneaking out. I'll let you know when I'm leaving."

It was with relief that she saw the kitchen door swing closed behind him and fled herself, a few minutes later, upstairs to sink gratefully into the corner of the sofa. Godzilla was fascinating, requiring all of her concentration. Her mind wouldn't spare a single moment for Ryan Crawford.

Ryan marched into the den, telling himself it didn't matter that Val had snuck out without telling him. So what if he found her company relaxing? Of greater importance was the fact that the boys had left all the lights on and—

He stopped short at the sight of the figure curled up asleep at one end of the sofa. Val hadn't left. What had the boys said that had made him think she had?

His movements slowed into silence as he took the videotape out of the VCR and turned all the equipment off. After putting the tape back in its case, he turned his attention back to Val, a soft smile tugging at the corners of his mouth as he shook his head. She must really have been tired. The boys had left all the lights on and the TV blaring, as they had quietly tiptoed off to bed like a small herd of elephants. Yet she had slept through it all.

A twinge of guilt seized his stomach. She had every right to be tired. She was the chief executive of a small but thriving company, and instead of relaxing this weekend, she was over here playing hostess.

He tried to tell himself that it was sympathy that kept his feet rooted to the floor and his hands at his sides. He knew how tired she must be and that he hated to wake her. But then realism and honesty prevailed. A host of emotions were raging within him, but sympathy wasn't one of them. He wasn't certain he wanted to put names to the others.

Val lay curled up in the corner of the sofa, her lips slightly parted and one arm up under her head. Her tough exterior had been shed like a suit of armor, showing Ryan a young, vulnerable woman. A woman just waiting for someone to lead her into the land of—

He frowned and brought himself back down to earth. She'd wind up with a stiff neck if somebody didn't wake her soon. He went over and shook her lightly by the shoulder. "Val," he said. "Val, wake up."

Her body slowly turned toward him. A soft moan escaped the damp parted lips and a frown scrambled to gain a foothold in her face. But her eyes stayed closed.

"Val," Ryan said as he shook her again, his voice growing sharper as his mind suggested other uses for his hand.

But then her eyes flew open and confusion filled them. She stared at him for a second, then sprang to her feet.

"Oh, I must have dozed off," she said, but then just as suddenly put one hand to her head and with the other searched for something to lean on. She sat down rather unsteadily on the arm of the sofa.

"Are you all right?" Ryan asked, taking her by the shoulders and helping her back down to the seat of the sofa.

She nodded. "I'm fine now. I think I just got up too fast."

"Good." He reluctantly removed his hands.

Ryan stood there looking at her. He saw confusion in her eyes, but he also saw other emotions that he wasn't sure he could or wanted to name.

"What time is it?" she asked, shaking her head and blinking some more.

"Almost two. That's two in the a.m."

Her eyes grew wide, scattering sleep like dishwater from a pan. "Oh, my gosh."

"I'm sorry," he said. "I thought you'd gone. The boys said you had, but I guess they meant you'd gone out like a light or something, so Ted and I kept working. It wasn't until I came up here to turn off the lights that I discovered you. I am sorry," he ended.

"That's okay," she replied, stifling a yawn. "Me and the kids had a nice time. They watched the movie and I sawed wood." She grinned ruefully. "It was probably just as well. I wouldn't have set a good example whining and crying during the scary parts."

"My parents never let me watch monster movies," Ryan said, pulling the hassock over to sit down. "I guess they thought I'd have nightmares and that it would stunt my growth or something like that."

"I don't think your kids are in any danger of nightmares. I heard more laughter than screams of fright." She reached down with her feet for her shoes but ended up trying to put them on the wrong feet.

He sorted them out for her. "I think you ought to just spend the night here," he said. "You don't look in any shape to drive."

"That's all right," Val said with a laugh. "I'm fine."

"You look like a zombie."

"Ah, back to compliments, are we?"

"A lovely zombie, but a zombie nonetheless."

She managed to get her shoes on and stood up. "I think I left my purse in the kitchen."

"You have somebody at home?" he asked.

"No, I live alone."

"No pets?"

"Two cats."

"Will they worry if you sleep here?"

"That's assuming they'd even notice I was gone, but I'm perfectly able to get myself home."

"Those are mean streets out there," he said.

"In Fort Wayne?" A highly disbelieving look filled her face. "As in Indiana?"

"Hey, a lot of things can happen. Assault, accident, dozing at the wheel."

"I'm rather overwhelmed by all this concern." There was only the slightest touch of sarcasm in her voice.

"My concern is strictly business," he said. "You're the only one in town willing to find me a housekeeper. I have to keep you able and healthy."

Val gave him a long, level look. The expression in her eyes was inscrutable. Ryan got the impression that putting the situation back on a businesslike level pushed her closer to staying.

"This is a big house," he pointed out. "We have a guest room that's downstairs and in the back, with its own bathroom. You can sleep in peace and not be bothered by anyone."

Her eyes seemed to cloud over with weariness again, or was she just giving in to it? "That sounds fine."

"Unless, of course, you'd like to see my bedroom," he said, possessed by an unknown demon.

She just shook her head, punctuating it with a yawn. "It had better wait until daylight. My night vision is rather poor."

"All the more reason for staying then," he said and took her arm. "Come on, I'll show you the room."

He led her downstairs, pleased for some reason that he'd convinced her to stay. He truly hadn't wanted her to drive home as groggy as she was, but he had to admit to himself that that was only part of it. The house seemed somehow warmer and safer with her here, more complete.

The guest room was on the other side of the kitchen, a bright little room that was smaller than he remembered. He opened up the sofa bed only to find it was sheetless.

"I'll get you some sheets and stuff," he said.

"Okay."

He was back in a few minutes with the bedclothes plus nightwear for her. "Here's one of Casey's nightshirts and a pair of my pajamas. I'm not sure either will fit but maybe between the two you can find something that works."

She took them from him. "They'll be fine."

"Or maybe I could—" He stopped, certain that he was rambling, and turned his attention to the bed.

"I could make that," she protested as he started to put the sheets on the bed.

"Nope, you're the guest."

She watched as he hurried to make the bed and fussed straightening out the wrinkles. "I'm going to wrinkle the sheets anyway," she said.

"Are you a restless sleeper?"

She chose not to answer. "Thank you," she said. "This will all be fine."

He hated to leave her. There was a gentleness, a vulnerability about her that made her presence special. It wasn't just a physical longing either, though that was certainly there. It was that sense that she could hold back the chaos, that somehow she held the key to a sunnier, brighter world. He suddenly realized she was staring at him, waiting for him to leave so she could go to bed.

"Well, see you in the morning," he said. What would it be like to greet the morning with her? To hold her all through the night and wake up ready to face a new day rather than dreading it?

"Good night," Val said softly. "Pleasant dreams."

"Right," he said, and told his feet to take him from the room, but somehow the message got mixed up. Without actually deciding to, he took a step closer to Val and took her in his arms.

Their lips met in a gentle caress; her body swayed slightly into his. The warmth, the softness of her touch awoke sweet memories; his heart flickered alive in ways that surprised him. It was like spring had come after a long, hard winter. His soul felt bathed in the sweet, silent peace of her presence. The night suddenly held no more fears.

But even as his heart warmed to the radiance of her touch, his mind pulled back. If he didn't fight against the lure of this woman's calm and restful soul his unwary feelings would lead him down paths he'd vowed never to take again. He gently released her, refusing to be stirred by the faint sparks of passion in her eyes left unguarded by weariness.

"Good night," he said. "Sleep well." Before she could respond he was gone, out in the hall where the cool shadows of the night would bring back his good sense. But would it also bring sleep?

Val washed her face before sinking onto the edge of the bed, trying to stifle a yawn as she pulled the pajamas over toward her. She could still feel the strength of Ryan's body against hers, still feel the pressure of his lips on hers. She hadn't wanted him to kiss her, her heart assured her worried mind. She hadn't wanted him to hold her and she would have protested his actions if he hadn't released her when he had. Sleepiness hadn't weakened her defenses.

She pushed aside Casey's nightshirt and unfolded Ryan's pajamas, putting on only the top. Its shoulders were big, but the length was comfortable. She crawled into bed, feeling warm and protected. It almost felt like being in his arms, but safer. Her eyes sagged closed but her lips curved into a smile as she drifted off to sleep. Dreaming about him wouldn't mean anything either. No reason for her mind to panic; she'd learned her lessons too well in the past to do anything foolish.

By morning, Val had come to her senses. What had she been thinking of, getting all soft and moony over his kiss last night? She should have taken her chances on the road rather than let her heart start escaping from behind its wall. She'd felt the strange power this home and this family had over her. She got up, vowing that she would be gone within the hour and this time would stay away.

The kids were up when she came out into the kitchen. They were preparing to eat some awful-looking cereal, so she made them crepes, which she filled with the leftover strawberries that had garnished the dessert tray the night before. Fixing breakfast was not breaking her vow, she pointed out to herself. Breakfast was the most important meal of the day, and besides, she was not running out of here like a coward.

"Good morning, Dad," Casey said as Val was serving up the second round of crepes.

She turned from the table and looked at Ryan's smiling face as he greeted his children. His usually unruly hair was combed, but she could see it took a great deal of effort on his part to keep it that way. Maybe fleeing would have been wise. She stiffened her spine.

"Hey, Dad," Richard said. "Miss Dennison is making skinny pancakes. They're really good."

Ryan looked at her. His eyes were tender, but she saw a hesitation in them that helped her relax slightly.

"You're a woman of many talents," he said. "Executive and now world-class chef."

Her heart wanted to warm to him, but her wits weren't dulled by sleep this morning. She was in control now. "There were a lot of strawberries left over from the dessert garnishes yesterday," she said. "So I made crepes. Would you like some?"

He sat down at the table. "If it's not too much trouble. I feel like we've imposed on you enough already."

She turned back to the stove. "No trouble." She'd make him some, then be on her way. Maybe it would stretch her hour a tad, but nothing to get alarmed about.

"We're done," the boys announced.

"Then put your dishes in the dishwasher," Casey said as she cleaned up her area of the table.

"And straighten up the living room," Val said over her shoulder. "Casey will check the porch for anything we missed last night. You do the same for the living room."

"Should we vacuum it?"

Val turned around and frowned at the boys, but they seemed serious. "Uh, Casey will decide if it needs it," she said.

"Okay."

Val stared as the three of them hurried off to their appointed tasks.

"That was very impressive," Ryan said. "What sort of threats did you use? I could use something new. My old ones are losing their punch."

"I never threaten people," she replied. "And they're nice kids."

"You've said that before. I thought you'd have learned your lesson by now."

That depended on which lesson he was referring to. The crepes were done, so she piled them on a plate and got herself another cup of coffee. She usually had only one cup in the morning, but this would give her something to do besides watch Ryan.

"They *are* nice kids," she repeated as she sat down.

He shrugged as he swallowed a mouthful. "Then how come I can't keep a housekeeper?" he asked.

"Maybe you're the problem," she said.

He laughed, then concentrated on his breakfast. Val sipped at her coffee, watching his hands as they cut the crepes and remembering how they had pressed against her back last night. The sight of his lips as they closed around his fork awoke memories of how they had felt touching hers. She shook off her daydreams.

"Actually I've gotten to know your kids pretty well over the past day or so," she said. "And they're not bad kids."

Ryan took a sip of coffee, then put his cup down. "Lively, maybe?"

Val shook her head. "More like scared." Questions clouded his eyes and she went on quickly. "You're more involved outside the home now," she pointed out.

His face turned a tad harder. "I really can't make it by working entirely at home."

"They know that," Val said. "That doesn't mean they can't worry."

"About what?"

"I'm sure they're afraid that they'll lose you."

Ryan looked down at his fingers. "Well, I can't guarantee immortality, but I'm sure going to try sticking around for a while."

"No, they're more afraid that they're going to lose you to your job or some woman."

He looked up at her. All softness was gone, banished and defeated by a hard determination.

"That'll never happen. They come first."

"Maybe you should tell them."

"I do." He shrugged. "But they're going to have to see that on their own, too. One of the reasons I'm expanding my business again is to take care of them better."

"You know that and I know that," Val said. "But they're just kids. They need to be reminded of that a little more often."

"I'll keep that in mind."

"It might also help if you did things with them on a regular basis."

He nodded again. "Yeah, show them that I'm not abandoning them entirely for the world of work."

"Given your type of work," Val said, "it would be a good idea if you scheduled events with them. Use your secretary to make sure that you do things with them."

He smiled broadly. "You mean, given my lack of organization."

Val returned his smile. "I didn't say that."

Still smiling, Ryan rose and cleaned off his place. "I'm a good boy, too," he said as he put his dishes in the dishwasher.

"Good," Val said as she stood up. It was getting a touch warmer in the kitchen. Time to go.

Suddenly Ryan was next to her, taking her free hand in both of his before she could move away. "Thank you for taking care of all of us."

Val pulled back slightly but he held her hand. "Hey," she said with a shrug, "you need it, we do it. That's my slogan, remember?"

"I sure do," he whispered as he kissed her gently on the cheek.

Val was out the door in less than a minute. She hadn't turned and run—a woman of dignity and maturity didn't bolt when kissed by a man—but neither did she linger. After polite but swift goodbyes to everyone, she was out of the house and in her car.

Lingering was just what she'd been doing too much of, she told herself as she backed out of the driveway. No more. She was going straight to the office now, even if it was Sunday morning. She would search those files until she found a housekeeper for the Crawfords.

Chapter Five

For Ryan, Monday started off with a bang, or more accurately a crash, as Robert dropped a carton of eggs on the floor while trying to make some of Val's "skinny pancakes." Then while Ryan was helping the boy wipe egg white up from the tile, the kids' grandparents called to see if Ryan had been able to make other arrangements for the summer. His father said they'd change their plans if he needed them, but Ryan told them to go ahead with their plans. After some scrambling around, he arranged for the kids to stay with the Fergusons across the street. He felt as if he'd been put through the wringer and hung out to dry by the time he reached the office, only to discover that it wasn't over yet. A construction crew had knocked out the power for his building and it was being lighted by auxiliary lights.

The phones were about the only thing still working. He dialed Val's office.

"I just barely got in," she said when he told her who it was. "I haven't had time to start looking for someone for you."

His conscience twinged. "I wasn't calling to bug you," he said. "I was calling to be restored to sanity." Now why had he admitted that, true though it might be?

Val laughed, not taking him seriously. "HSI offers a lot of services, but I've never been asked for that one."

"That's because no one ever had a day like mine."

"It's not even ten o'clock."

He cradled the phone on his shoulder and leaned back in his chair, the tensions of the morning floating away like an early-morning fog under sunshine. "Robert dumped a carton of eggs on the floor."

"A whole dozen?"

"Twelve shells smashed into tiny pieces. Twelve egg yolks running all over my kitchen floor and twelve egg whites lying in wait to make me slip and fall."

"Should be glad you don't buy those dozen-and-a-half packages."

The fog dissipated slightly and he smiled. "All right, so you found the silver lining in that one. There's more. I had to ask the neighbors to watch the kids."

"At least they're in their own neighborhood."

"And the power's out in my building."

"Gives you time to relax and regroup before you start your day."

His smile went deeper than his lips; it invaded his soul and spread sunshine and warmth. "You really do provide a complete service, don't you?"

Her gentle chuckling came over the wires. "I haven't found a housekeeper for you yet."

"But you will." The lights flickered on. "The lights are back on. Did you manage that for me, too?"

"No, it's the gods telling you to get to work."

"Yes, ma'am." A strange reluctance came over him. He didn't want to put the phone down. "You'll call when you have somebody?"

"I promise. It's my number one priority."

"Right. I'll be waiting."

The rest of the day went as smoothly as Val's running of the party Saturday night. He must have gotten all his bad luck out of the way early in the day, he told himself. He left work early and took the kids miniature golfing, then out to dinner.

He awoke Tuesday to rain, but breakfast went without a hitch—only half a glass of orange juice got spilled. The kids were again sent over to the Fergusons with the promise that it shouldn't be for much longer. They assured him it was fine. They were so cooperative, in fact, that it set Ryan to thinking as he drove down to the office. He dialed Val's number the first thing.

"More broken eggs?" she asked.

"No, no, everything's great," he said. "I was just thinking as I drove down here that maybe I've been making too big a deal about needing a disciplinarian. After all, Mrs. Huntsen didn't work out at all and how much more of a disciplinarian can you get?"

"Mrs. Staples was the opposite."

"Too nice," he said. "I need someone in-between."

"You need a miracle."

"Got any in store?"

"I'm trying."

He sighed and stared at the rivers of rain running down the window. "We sure are lucky to have you helping us out," he said.

"That's what you pay me for," she reminded him.

"You can't buy the kind of service you've been giving us," he said, but even as he said the words, his heart shied away from their seriousness. "Or should I look into a second mortgage to pay your bill?"

"That ought to cover it," she said with a laugh a little too hearty and a little too long. "That and any money you've got set aside for the kids' college."

He relaxed even more. She shied away from seriousness just as he did. Maybe that was why he felt so at ease with her. There was no pressure, no easing closer to threaten the rocky foundation he was living on at the moment.

"Look, I've got to run," she said. "My nine o'clock appointment just came in. Keep your fingers crossed. She might be just what you want."

"Fingers and toes at your service," Ryan promised.

Things went even better that day than the day before. Casey fixed spaghetti for dinner; then they all watched some television together. Chaos was ebbing away, little by little.

Was it just the lull before the storm? he asked himself Wednesday morning. He had an early meeting—the only time he could schedule it—but Casey was moody and didn't want any breakfast. The twins were lazy, dawdling over their cereal, so that by the time he'd gotten the kids to the Fergusons, everyone was good and grumpy.

Damn. He couldn't take much more of these ups and downs. A faint memory of Val's calm demeanor teased his mind, but he pushed it aside. He was not about to call her just to be coaxed into a better mood; he wasn't dependent on her for such things. He did wonder though about that interview she'd had yesterday. Had it been someone with promise?

He tried to turn his thoughts aside and concentrate on his meeting. The first chance he got though, he called her. "Val, it's Ryan. All my eggs are broken and the house is drowning in spilled milk."

"Uh, Mr. Crawford?" It wasn't Val's voice. "This is Marcie, Val's secretary. She's not available right now. Can I take a message?"

Not available? Of course, how presumptuous of him to assume that she'd always be there waiting for his call. He felt his face redden, and he stiffened his mental spine. "I just wondered how her search for a housekeeper for us was going," he said.

"I'm sure she'll call as soon as she has something to report," Marcie said, the perfect professional.

"Yes, of course."

"I'll tell her you called though."

"Right, thanks."

He went to another meeting, his black mood of the morning only getting blacker. It wasn't that he thought she had nothing to do but answer his calls, but he was paying her to find them a housekeeper and he wished she would hurry up and do it. His mood got even darker, if that was possible, when he got out of the meeting to learn she had called back a half hour earlier. What did she think, that he had nothing to do but wait by the phone?

The irrationality of his thoughts was not lost on him, but it only made him gloomier. Just as another set of traded messages did. Damn.

The phone rang in the middle of the afternoon, when it was Val's turn to call, and he snatched it up irritably. It wasn't Val, but Jan Ferguson.

"Robert fell out of the tree in the backyard," she told Ryan. "I'm taking him in to the emergency room, but you'll need to authorize treatment."

"I'll be right there."

By the time he reached the hospital, Ryan was almost a basket case himself. He couldn't cancel his late afternoon meeting because the client was driving up from Kentucky, so he ended up conducting it by telephone as Robert went to have his wrist x-rayed.

It was almost dinnertime when they left the hospital. Robert's sprained wrist was wrapped in a soft cast. A silent dinner was followed by a long evening spent trying to write a report while the kids watched television. Ryan fumed. Val had never gotten ahold of him. What was happening in his housekeeper search? Or had she abandoned him as the gods seemed to have done?

He called her home only to be greeted by an answering machine. It was the last straw and his anger exploded. "This is Ryan Crawford," he snapped. "I need a housekeeper. Now, if not sooner."

He slammed down the phone and stomped off to bed, spending the night in restless tossing and turning. It wasn't Val's fault that Robert had fallen out of a tree. Even the most vigilant housekeeper might not have prevented that. It wasn't her fault either that he was feeling overwhelmed by everything. But the acknowledgment didn't make sleep come any easier.

The phone was ringing as Val unlocked her office door the next morning; she grabbed up the receiver before the answering machine kicked in. Not everyone reacted well to talking to a machine, she was learning.

"Val? It's Ryan." His voice was quiet, tentative. Apologetic.

She sank into a chair with a grin on her face. "Boy, am I lucky I got in when I did. One more ring and the answering machine would have taken the call."

"Val." Slightly more spirit in his voice.

"I mean, you wouldn't believe how upset some people get when talking to an answering machine."

"Val." Tentative was a description of the past.

"Of course, it does make for interesting listening, especially when you get home late from a Chamber of Commerce meeting."

"Damn it, Val, will you let me apologize?" he snapped, then bit into silence. "I'm sorry," he muttered a moment later, his voice back to meek and mild.

She just laughed. "No problem. I just figured you had a bad day."

"Boy, did I ever. Robert fell out of a tree and they rushed him to the hospital. He just sprained his wrist, but we didn't know that until they x-rayed."

"Poor little guy. How is he today?"

"They're all happy and cheerful, ready to fall out of more trees or break more eggs."

"You don't sound as good."

"I don't rebound as fast as I used to."

"Poor baby," she cooed, then felt something change. She wasn't sure what it was, but she felt a tension in the air, a current that tightened her stomach.

"Let me take you to lunch," Ryan said suddenly. "I feel I owe you something for my outburst."

"You don't owe me anything."

"I'd like to take you to lunch."

"On nice days like this I usually have a yogurt and a long walk."

"Then I'll have yogurt and a long walk, too. Is noon all right with you?"

Why am I skittish all of a sudden? she wondered. It was the combination of him, his house and his family that had seemed so dangerous in the past. The myth of the happy family, a place of belonging and acceptance that had awakened strange longings within her. She told herself she had nothing to worry about in sharing a noontime with him.

"Noon would be fine."

In spite of her inner scoldings she agreed with less enthusiasm than she thought polite, but as much as she could muster. Which was silly, she scolded herself all morning long. Company for lunch would be fun, a nice change from her solitary strolls or a snack gobbled down at her desk. Ryan Crawford wanted a housekeeper, nothing more.

And housekeepers was what they talked about when he came by her office. After getting some yogurt from the little grocery store down the block, they went across the street to a riverside park, sat on a bench and ate.

"She seems really perfect." Val was telling him about a woman she'd interviewed two days before. "Tough but loving and with a great sense of humor. All that I'm waiting for is the reference check."

"And how long will that take?"

"Another few days at most."

He nodded and frowned down at the yogurt carton. "This is all you eat and you manage not to faint dead away by two o'clock?"

"Hey, it's nourishing."

"So is a pea, but one doesn't fill you up."

She got to her feet. "We need to start walking. That'll make you forget your hunger pangs."

"I doubt that."

The day was warm. A gentle breeze mussed her hair and relaxed her soul as they started to walk along the riverbank. She'd been right—there was nothing to fear from having lunch with Ryan. He was fun to be with, not a threat to be feared. They passed behind a fast-food restaurant.

"Don't you think we ought to stop to rest?" Ryan said. "I'm not used to all this exercise."

"We've walked about a hundred yards so far," Val pointed out. "You can handle a little more than that without folding."

"You're a cruel woman," he muttered. "Maybe your soul cries out for yogurt, but mine needs a hamburger, french fries, a strawberry shake and a big chocolate candy bar to keep my spirits up."

"That's awful," Val laughed.

"No, no," he insisted. "I have that combination a lot. It's very tasty."

"Sounds like you need a housekeeper to look after you more than the kids do."

She'd meant it as a joke, a little teasing between friends, for they surely were that in spite of the business relation that linked them. But his face sagged into a sweet sadness and they walked in silence for a long moment.

"You're probably right," he finally replied, his voice quiet.

"I'm sorry," Val said. She hadn't meant to remind him of the pain of his past.

"Hey, no problem. I'm a big boy. I'm over Maggie's death." He picked a napkin up off the sidewalk and, utilizing a modified hook shot, threw it into the trash can.

"Are you?" she asked. There were pains in the past that she'd never be free of.

"Yeah, I am." He paused. "Sort of."

Silence came between them, walking along with them until they crossed the bridge.

"I guess some people go through life living with each other but not really together," Ryan said. "But then there are others, like Maggie and I were. After being married almost fifteen years, we were almost as one."

Val felt a bit of a lump in her throat and decided it would be better if she didn't say anything.

"When she was gone it was like half my heart and lungs were cut out," he said. "I could breathe enough to exist, but not enough to live."

"I lost both my parents when I was a kid," Val said. "But I imagine losing your life partner is even harder."

He shrugged. "I don't know. Probably like the difference between losing an arm and losing a leg. Both hurt and both leave you handicapped, only in different ways."

Had she been handicapped by her parents' deaths? She'd always felt more handicapped by the bitterness in the air, the sense that their love had died long ago and they were only going through the motions for her sake. But yes, their deaths had hurt her, and rocked the boat of her security, which was so much a part of love.

"I guess it depends on how close you were to the other person," she said.

Ryan nodded. "Maggie and I were probably too close."

"Isn't that like saying that you loved each other too much?" she asked. "Is there such a thing?"

Another shrug and his hands ran through his hair, mussing it more than the breeze ever could. Val felt the urge to smooth it down, to smooth down all the rumpled spots life had left on his road, but she just balled up her hands and jammed them into her pants pockets. There was nothing special in her desire to smooth Ryan's hair, she told herself. Just a genetic predisposition that all females were afflicted with.

"It was great when we were together," Ryan went on. "But it hurt like hell when she was gone."

It had hurt when her parents died, and again when Danny left, but neither had left the emptiness, the aching, that giving up the baby had. Never a day went by that she didn't think of him, wish circumstances had been different, pray that he was safe and well.

"The kids were the only thing that kept me going," Ryan said. "Taking care of them made me go through the routine activities of life until I wanted to do it for myself."

"Sometimes you need someone or something outside yourself," she said softly. For her it had been her work. Throw yourself into it until your body was too tired for your mind to think.

"But I'm never going to hurt like that again. I'm never going to have that type of relationship again," he said. "People who don't know what they're talking about say that the good times make up for the bad, but that's only true if the bad comes first, so that the good times wipe out the memories. Like having a baby. The joy of holding the child wipes out the pain of birth."

She'd never held her son; she'd been advised against it. Avoid the bonding process and avoid the pain. Ryan was right: Those who know nothing are full of supposed wisdom.

She realized they had stopped walking and were standing at the rail, overlooking the river. Turning, she faced him. "So now you're staying away from fire, so that you don't get burned."

"That's my plan," he said firmly, then added, "It's not that I don't date. I'm just not going to get involved like that ever again."

"Some relationships can be very distracting," Val agreed, and turned back to stare at the water. A leaf had fallen in and was dancing gently along the current. "It's almost like you have to set up rules right in the beginning. Men just can't believe that I'm not out there looking for Prince Charming."

"But you aren't?" It was half question, half statement.

She shook her head. The urge to confide was strong. Something in the warm, summer sun made her throw her normal caution and reticence into the swirling, muddy waters below her.

"My parents weren't particularly happy," she said carefully. "So I don't buy the automatic 'happily ever after' endings. Then my teenage years in foster homes were not exactly stable, so I value security and stability above all else. I've always figured my business was a better bet in the long run than hoping some man will support me."

"You've done well with it," he said. "Your commitment shows."

"It was a better investment of my time than a relationship."

Ryan turned from his contemplation of the river, his eyes warm with sadness. "Somebody hurt you but good," he said.

His sympathy surprised her. She looked away as if the catch in her voice might reappear if he could look into her eyes.

"I didn't mean to sound quite so bitter," she said, forcing a laugh into her words. "I'm not. Just careful and cautious. The problem is, you're too easy to talk to. Words just seem to come out of my mouth from nowhere with you."

He laughed. "Just like the kids, it's all my fault."

"Hey, it's got to be somebody's and it sure isn't mine."

He took her arm and they strolled back the way they'd come. "You're right though, you know," he said. "Not that I'm so easy to talk to, but words do seem to come from nowhere. I find myself saying things to you I never expected to say to anyone."

"Should we be worried?"

"No, it's great. We're simpatico."

"Our personal karmas are compatible."

He grinned at the quote from their first meeting. "Come to think of it, I guess all my calls this week were part of that. I was looking for a sympathetic ear."

"I thought you were looking for a housekeeper."

"Only partly. I think I'd discovered how great it was to have someone to talk to. Someone who wouldn't misinterpret every other word as a prelude to everlasting love."

"Oh, you mean I could have read last night's phone call that way?" she asked with a grin, then grew more somber. "I guess I sort of skimped on friendships along the way. I was so careful to avoid other relationships that I forgot how nice a friend can be."

"Or how safe."

They were coming to the end of the river walkway. In a moment they would take the steps up to the street level; then Ryan would go on to his office while she would cross the park and make her way back to her office. She was sorry to see the lunch hour end; it had been much more enjoyable than she'd expected.

"So what do you think? Want to catch a play or a movie once in a while?" he asked. "No strings attached, just two friends out for the evening?"

"You play tennis?" she asked. "I think the thing I miss most is a tennis partner."

"I'm reasonable at tennis. How are you at bike riding?"

They'd started up the steps.

"Haven't done it in a while, but that's one thing you aren't ever supposed to forget, isn't it?"

"I'd like to take the kids down to Brown County in the fall," he said. "You know when all the leaves color. You could come along if you want."

"That would be fun," she agreed. "I bet they'd love all those old covered bridges."

They stopped at the top of the stairs. The air was light between them, ripe with the promise of friendship. She smiled at him.

"Well, I'd better get back," she said.

"Me, too," Ryan said. "If I don't finish that Oberlin College proposal today, my secretary will wring my neck."

"Well, I can't help you with that. Though HSI would do a good job of cleaning up your office after your secretary finishes the mayhem."

They both laughed, then parted with friendly waves. This was definitely the best lunch she'd had in years. She started across the park unable to keep the smile in her heart from showing on her lips.

Suddenly there were shouting voices and three boys came racing along on bikes. They were gangly, pimply-faced youths, lost in that chasm between childhood and manhood called adolescence. Their voices cracked and their manners were boisterous, at times bordering on the boorish. They looked to be junior high school students, about thirteen, the age at which only a mother could love them and then only if she concentrated on it.

Val stopped and stared at them as they sped by her. The easy mood that Ryan left her with ran and hid like a frightened child as the black clouds of gloom descended. Her son would be about their age now.

She'd never named him, not even in the most secret recesses of her memory. To name was to possess and cherish. She could do neither. At nineteen, she had had the body to give life to another but not the resources to maintain that life. She'd cried her heart out after she'd signed the adoption release papers, but never with a thought of changing her mind. If only the circumstances could have been changed. If Danny had only loved her. If she'd had a family to help her. But love had dictated her path, love for the feisty little boy who deserved better than a minimum-wage life. Who deserved two parents to love him and give him all the things that children were supposed to have.

It had sounded so right, so mature at nineteen. What Val hadn't known was that she'd never get over the emptiness. That her heart would be frozen with love for her unnamed, unheld son. That her life would pass but never move on.

That weepy girl who'd left the maternity ward alone had built a good life for herself. She'd worked hard as a maid in that old hotel and things had taken off from there.

Val had tried to deny the emptiness that ate at her, but that just made things worse. The more she denied it, the more her son made his absence felt. Thoughts of him would first appear in that quiet time between the shedding of the day's activities and sleep; then he pushed into her dreams and moved into her waking hours.

Externally Val remained the same, but internally she was a bundle of nerves. Was his presence the result of her guilt? Or was there some truth to theories of psychic phenomena and mental telepathy? Maybe he was in trouble and calling for her help. The pain had become almost unbearable, until she'd had to do something.

She'd hired a private detective, setting him on the case. The detective had run into the dead ends and closed legal files that she had expected, but she still felt better. She was doing something and one day would succeed. One day she would find her son again and, just in seeing him, would put aside the emptiness forever.

The boys had long since disappeared amid the lunchtime crowd in the park and Val continued on her way to her office. It was great that she and Ryan had stepped into each other's lives. He didn't want to make a commitment again and she couldn't, not as long as her heart had room only for thoughts of her son. She had no room for love in her life. Her heart was already overflowing with it, but it was all for her lost little boy and no one else.

Chapter Six

Val smiled as she saw the silver Ford Taurus hurry into the early Sunday morning quiet of the parking lot of her town house complex. It was more than a week since she and Ryan had taken their luncheon walk, a week punctuated with several phone calls and a number of crossed fingers as his family adjusted to their new housekeeper. The week had progressed from tentatively good to routinely great, so Ryan was moving the kids up to the lake today, wanting to get them settled before the Fourth of July next weekend. Val had been invited along for the day.

Now she sat, chin in hand, and waited until the car skidded to a stop in front of her. Ryan scrambled out of the car, brushing at his already unkempt locks.

"We're late," Robert of the bandaged wrist called from the back window.

"Daddy couldn't find his shoes," Richard added.

Ryan glared over his shoulder at them. "Give me a chance to apologize myself, will you?" His smile was sheepish as he turned back to her. "Sorry I'm late."

"Couldn't find your shoes, huh?"

"I knew where they were, " he insisted. "We're late because we had to stop at the drugstore and buy some insect repellant because someone used up a whole bottle last night."

"I had to, Dad," Robert protested. "There were bugs all over the screen and they were coming in every time I opened the door."

"Maybe we should have stayed in, too, then," Ryan said with exaggerated sweetness, then smiled back at Val. "Anyway, I'm sorry we're late."

"Don't worry about it," she said, standing up. "If you'd have been on time I would have dropped dead from surprise."

The boys collapsed into a heap in the back seat of the car. They couldn't be seen but their laughter could certainly be heard.

"Nice group I'm taking to the lake," Ryan muttered as he tossed Val's bag into the trunk.

Val kissed him lightly on the cheek. "Yes, we are, and I forgive you for being late."

A frown creased his forehead and a smokelike haze clouded his eyes. Val thought it was best to change the tone and walked over to the passenger-side of the door. "Where's Casey?"

"She's riding up with Mrs. Ricco." Ryan opened the door for Val and she tucked herself in. "They're driving her station wagon and it's filled to the rafters with stuff. I think Casey figures she's riding shotgun."

There was an ease to Ryan's voice, a sense of laughter that made it unnecessary to ask how the new housekeeper was working out. As far as he was concerned, the woman was obviously great. Val turned to the twins, sitting amid bags in the backseat. "So how do you guys like Mrs. Ricco?"

"She's nice."

"She laughs all the time."

"Even in the presence of rubber snakes," Ryan added.

Two little faces grinned sheepishly, miniature replicas of their father's face just a moment before. A tightness came to Val's stomach at the realization, a knowing that was somehow tinged with sadness. She turned back around and fastened her seat belt as Ryan pulled out of the parking lot.

"It sure is a great day to go to a lake," she said brightly. "Sunny, warm and lots of food in the picnic hamper."

"Food?" Ryan echoed. "Were we supposed to be bringing food?"

The boys dissolved into giggles again, but by the time they were reaching the outskirts of the city, they were talking her into playing a game.

"But I told you I was awful at games," she protested.

"This one's easy," Robert assured her.

"That's what you said about charades."

"Auto bingo is real easy," Richard told her, stressing the "real" into a four syllable word.

Val just glanced at Ryan. His lips were trying hard to be serious, but his eyes were laughing with her. "What can I say? They like you," he teased.

"Or have decided I'm easy to win against," she muttered.

"Hey, us Crawford men are honorable," Ryan insisted. "We're honest, loyal and true-blue. We don't have hidden motives behind our invitations."

"What a relief!" she mocked, though her heart smiled at the reaffirmation of their friendship. There were no hidden strings here, no traps for the unwary to fall into.

"Okay, here's your card," Robert said, apparently taking her moment of silence for consent. "Whenever you see something on your card, call it out and then close the little door over it."

"Gas station!" Richard called out.

"Hey, we didn't start yet."

"Yes, we did."

"No, we didn't."

"Boys." Ryan's voice was definite and the backseat bickering stopped. "We'll start once we cross this intersection."

Val sent a sideways grin at Ryan. "You left out competitive when you were describing the Crawford men."

"Can't give all our secrets away," he said, but his smile was so open, so friendly, that she knew there'd be no secrets between them. There was lots they didn't know about each other yet, but no secrets.

They sped along and soon the barns of antiques, strip malls and cemeteries gave way to farmland, open fields covered with lines of greenery. She found a water pump and a silo for her auto-bingo card but wasn't even trying to keep up with the twins. At the rate they were calling out horses, picnic benches and doghouses, you'd think they were each filling up two cards. Not that she wasn't every bit as competitive as the next person, but somehow that didn't apply here with Ryan's family. She could relax and be herself.

Soon Ryan turned off the state highway onto a narrow country road. "You'd better get cutting if you want to win," he told her.

"I can live with coming in third," she said, but claimed the fire station she glimpsed up ahead as hers, to the groans of two fire-station-needing boys.

In another few miles, Ryan turned off onto a dirt lane that seemed to disappear into a thick stand of honeysuckle bushes, but actually opened up onto a large yard, populated with several oak trees, old enough to have shaded the first white men who visited the Northwest Territory before it was cut up into states. A square, two-story white cottage, covered with more love than paint, faced the lake.

"This lake was one of the first in the area developed for summer vacations," Ryan said. "The cottages aren't as fancy as those in the newer developments, but it has a charm all its own, especially with the large lots."

Val looked around the yard. Trees and bushes filled the back and sides, leaving only a broad path to the lake open. Muted voices, children's laughter, and hints of other cottages buried in the greenery were the only indications of other life around.

Mixed in with the rustle of a light breeze through the leaves, Val heard the call of ancient forest nymphs, who had probably settled here even before the Indians came, ordering her to remove her shoes. She obeyed without question. The gods were obviously pleased, for when she stepped out of the car the longish grass, filled with a soothing coolness, wrapped her feet and sucked all the cares and tension of the modern-day world out of her body.

"This is beautiful." She sighed.

Ryan shrugged and his lips parted to speak, but Casey came spilling out of the house before words came filling out of his mouth. The girl's eyes had the smudged rainbow effect of an early attempt at makeup.

"We beat you," she cried, and flung her arms around Ryan, before smiling a hello at Val. "Wait till you see the place. It's great."

The boys apparently were taking that as a direct order and were poised for flight, before Ryan put a hand on a shoulder of each. "I think unloading the car comes first."

Their faces fell, but then they perked up as they both reached for Val's bag. She was about to say she'd carry it herself, but the two of them were already scrambling for it, making the task into a joint project. Val looked a little dubiously at their tugging and pulling, but decided that the handles were strong enough to tolerate the efforts of two ten-year-old boys. She grabbed another bag from the backseat and followed Casey into the house.

"We got here about an hour ago so we've got most of the other stuff sort of put away."

Val brought the bag into the kitchen where Mrs. Ricco was scrubbing out cabinets.

"Need any help?" she asked the older woman.

She stopped cleaning for a moment to frown at Val. "Why does everybody want to take over my kitchen?" she asked, her frown slipping into a grin. "The first time through, I clean. Want it done right, do it yourself. I'll give everybody a turn next month, don't worry."

She went back to her cleaning, so Casey tugged at Val's arm, leading her down a hallway. "You can use my room to change into your bathing suit," she said. "The bathroom's down the hall."

She opened the first door into a small bedroom with two unmade twin beds occupying most of the space. A battered chest of drawers was under the window, but the place was clean and the air wafting in the open window smelled of pine trees and summer.

Casey sat down on one of the beds as Val pulled her swimsuit and toweling robe out of her bag. "This room has two beds," the girl said. "So you can sleep with me."

"I can't stay the night," Val said. "I have to get to work early tomorrow."

"I know that. I mean like when you come up on Saturday sometime and you don't want to drive up again on Sunday."

Val just smiled, not certain though why Casey was assuming she'd be coming up often.

"I mean, if Daddy doesn't invite you to stay over, I could."

That surprised Val. She'd never had someone who so actively wanted to be her friend before. She wasn't sure she knew how to do it. What kind of rules were there for friendships with thirteen-year-old-girls? Was Casey looking for a mother substitute? The idea was at once terrifying and appealing to Val.

"How's Mrs. Ricco working out?" Val asked. Surely the older woman was a more suitable guide through the perils of adolescence.

"All right," Casey said with a shrug.

Val's heart sank. She'd thought the woman perfect.

"I mean, she's nice and everything," Casey assured her, letting Val's heart begin to beat again. "But she keeps wanting to iron all my clothes and doesn't believe me when I tell her nobody irons their cotton shirts."

"Well, let's say no other teenagers do," Val corrected with a gentle laugh. "This blouse I have on is cotton and I admit to ironing it last night."

Casey shrugged with a good-natured grin. "And then she says that she's going to teach me how to cook because all women have to be able to cook, which Daddy says is archaic, that everybody—man or woman—should be able to cook for themselves. So she agreed to start teaching the twins too, but really easy stuff like hot dogs.''

"They are younger than you," Val pointed out, "and they have to start someplace."

"I guess," Casey said, lying back on the bed to stare at the ceiling. "She keeps the bread in the freezer so we have to defrost it slice by slice when we want some."

Val sighed and sat down on the other bed. "She's got her own ways," she told the girl gently. "She's a good person, but she's not going to do things the same way your mother did."

Casey sat up, her eyes roaming the floor rather than meet Val's. "I'm being a brat, aren't I?"

"No, you're being human. Every change Mrs. Ricco makes is a reminder of how much *your* life has changed. You wish it could be just the same as it was before, even though you know it can't be. Give yourself time."

Casey peeked a glance at Val, a flash of blue and black. "She clucks at me when I try to wear makeup."

Val laughed. She couldn't help herself, but Casey appeared not to take offense. "I cluck too," Val said. "You just don't hear me."

"Lots of girls my age wear makeup."

"Lots of girls your age aren't redheads with fair skin. You can't wear makeup suited for a brunette."

"Oh." The girl looked deflated.

"If your father agrees, I'll take you out one of these days and we'll get some more suitable stuff."

"Will you?" Casey squealed and flung herself at Val. "Oh, wow. That's great."

"Only if your father agrees," Val warned her, gently trying to extricate herself. "And only if you wash off what you have on now."

"Sure." Casey bounced to her feet and was out the door in a flash.

"See you outside."

Val took a deep breath and changed quickly, putting her robe on over her swimsuit, then hurrying outside. She stopped on the deck overlooking the backyard. Casey was already down at the water's edge playing with the twins, while Ryan was carrying a tray laden with glasses and a pitcher of lemonade to the picnic table. He looked fit and trim in his swimming trunks, every bit as magnificent as she'd suspected he'd look. He was solid muscle, dusted with a fine coating of brown hair. Her eyes ran over his shoulders and down his arms and a warmth flushed her cheeks. Friends could recognize good looks, she assured herself, and walked slowly down to join him.

"Ah, the miracle worker," he said by way of greeting. "Want a lemonade?"

"Love one." She took the glass and sat across from him at the bench, her eyes safely watching the condensation form on the glass. "What miracle am I being given credit for this time?" She let her eyes slide up to meet his, being careful not to get sidetracked along the journey.

"The healing of my daughter's eyes," he said and shook his head. "She looked like somebody'd beat her up."

"Not quite. It was just makeup."

He nodded. "So I realized, but hadn't the faintest idea how to tell her tactfully it looked atrocious. What'd you do? Hog-tie her and scrub it off?"

"Talk about tact." Val just laughed, her self-consciousness about Ryan's appearance burning off like dew under the morning sun. "No, I just suggested that redheads need different makeup from brunettes."

"And offered to help her choose some."

"If you didn't mind," Val added quickly.

"No. Though I'm sure Mrs. Ricco would take her if you don't have the time."

Val watched off toward the lake as the kids splashed in the shallow water. The sunlight glittered and danced on the surface of the water as a sailboat glided off in the distance. She took a deep breath and felt peaceful.

"I think it's best to let Casey choose her own mother substitutes," she said, then frowned and brought her eyes back to Ryan. "Not that I'm trying to be one."

He reached across the table to take her hand. His touch was strong, but not clinging. A reassurance of the pact they'd made.

"I don't care what kind of names you call things by. I'm only glad you're willing to help her out when she needs someone."

Val moved her hand, not to escape his but so that she was holding his as well. "She likes Mrs. Ricco, but she's having problems right now accepting anyone in any of the positions her mother used to hold. The more people she has to turn to, the easier she'll accept their intrusion in her life."

His eyes darkened. "Is that what you did to get over the death of your parents? Turned to all the people around you?"

"I guess," she said, though she hadn't. She'd turned away from them all, choosing rather to lock her heart away where it was safe. But, then, she hadn't had the constant of home and family that Casey had. The girl thought everything had changed in her life, but it hadn't, and those things that were the same would pull her through.

"The water looks inviting," Val said. "Is it deep?"

"About six feet at its deepest. Not quite up to ocean standards, but then there are no sharks to hide. Want to take a dip?"

"Sure." But even as they stood up, the old self-consciousness returned. They were just friends and her bathing suit was hardly revealing by today's standards, but still her hands moved awfully slowly when taking the robe off.

"It sure is good to have you here," Ryan said.

Her eyes came up to his and a spark seemed to pass between them. An elemental awareness that he was a man and she a woman. Strange hungers gripped her, longings tortured her resolve. Friends they might vow to be, but just what did friendship include these days?

Her hands had a sudden urge to touch and explore, her body had a sudden need to be held. She wondered what it would be like to rest in his arms, to have the luxury of someone else to lean on sometimes. Would his lips be as firm and demanding as they appeared, would his hands be as possessive as she'd want?

What was all this? she asked herself. They were friends, unemotional, uncommitted friends. Why was her silly heart suddenly feigning weakness?

Maybe Ryan was having trouble too, for even as the intensity in his eyes grew, he turned away, staring out at the lake. "We share that platform out there with the other neighboring cottages, so you can use it if you want."

"Okay." They started walking down to the lake, acting casual but feeling the tenseness in the air.

Casey saw them coming and called out, "Dad, want to have a race out to the float?"

"Sure." Ryan turned to Val. "You game?"

"Not yet," she said. "Maybe later." When her heart had regained its strength.

So she spent some time with Robert, who still wasn't allowed to use his sprained wrist much, then joined Mrs. Ricco, who was grilling hot dogs for their lunch. By late afternoon Val was feeling sufficiently lazy and swam out to the platform. It was warm and wonderful there as she stretched out in the sun. She closed her eyes to the glare and let the day's peace surround her.

She was making too much of the physical attraction between her and Ryan. It was a normal, natural thing for two unattached adults to experience and it didn't mean that either of them had changed their mind about the essence of their relationship. Ryan was still a friend, someone she could talk to, someone who knew how to listen.

She felt the float move and opened her eyes as Ryan climbed up onto it. "I was sent out here to check if you had any sunscreen," he said. "The kids didn't want you to get sunburned."

"I'm fine," she assured him. "I burn a bit, but not in a matter of a few minutes."

"You've been lying out here for over a half hour."

Val sat up partially and stared at him. "No, It can't have been that long."

"I guess you fell asleep." His lopsided smile assured her that he wasn't joking. "They don't allow any powerboats on this lake, so it's real easy to nod off around here."

Ryan lay down next to her and closed his eyes. His tanned skin gleamed with wetness, the muscles tight and hard just beneath the surface. His leg accidentally brushed hers and her skin felt scalded. Heat raged over her, starting from the spot he'd touched but not stopping until her whole body seemed afire. She edged away from him carefully, so as not to rock the float and make her movement obvious.

"Robert's pushing for another game of charades after dinner," Ryan said. "He claims they never really won the other game because you quit early."

Though his voice seemed tighter than normal, the words were hardly the stuff of seduction. She relaxed and let the gentle movement of the water still her nerves. "That game was called on account of darkness," she said.

Ryan opened one eye. "On account of darkness?"

"Sure, the darkness of my mind that couldn't figure anything out."

He smiled. "I see. So does that mean you're agreeable to a rematch?"

The fire was out for the moment, or at least smoldering down low, but she knew better than to give it fuel to burn again. "Actually, I was hoping we wouldn't get back too late. I've got a long week ahead of me."

"Okay. We'll postpone the rematch to another time." His eyes were soft, contented even, as they glowed with a strangely deep fire.

Val got to her feet. "About that race you challenged me to," she said. "Last one to shore's a rotten egg."

"Hey," he protested, even as she made a shallow dive into the water.

The cool water surrounded and blessed her, bringing back her senses as she swam toward shore. She could feel Ryan behind her but only laughed inside. It had been too long since she'd really had a friend and she was just making too big a deal out of it.

"I had a very pleasant day," Val said. "Thank you for inviting me."

Ryan kept his eyes on the dark road before him. "I'm glad to hear that. Sorry about the boys though."

Val laughed. It was such a pleasant laugh that started from someplace deep within her throat. "A rubber snake is no big deal."

"You did jump when you found it."

"I had to," Val protested. "If I didn't, they would have carried a bitter disappointment in their hearts for the rest of their lives. They'd grow up into misogynists and it would be all my fault."

"Right," he mocked, then lapsed into a comfortable silence.

Val didn't have any children of her own, but she sure seemed to understand his. The boys almost split a gut, laughing and rolling around after she'd found the rubber snake in her chair, but their hilarity was short-lived. Their laughter sure changed when she put ice cubes down their backs once they'd gotten dressed again. Yep, she sure did understand kids.

Maybe even better than he did. Ah, that was dumb. She was the one who told him to give some special times to them. He did, and things got straightened out, quickly he might add. In fact, it looked like he was more mopey than his kids when they parted.

If the truth be known, his kids didn't appear to be sad at all. All three cheerfully bid him goodbye, then immediately went back to helping Mrs. Ricco make french donuts. Munchies for late evening television watching the housekeeper had called them.

That couldn't be what was bothering him. After all, he was the one who was concerned his kids were clinging too tightly to him. After searching so long for the ideal housekeeper, why would he be upset now that he had found her and his kids were happy? Aw hell, maybe he just didn't know what he wanted.

"A penny for your thoughts?"

"You'll have to do better than that, lady," he said, forcing a growl in his voice. "I don't come that cheap."

"Goodness," she said, with that special laugh of hers. "You're a rather sensitive fellow."

He didn't answer for a moment, concentrating on turning onto the state highway that would take them back to Fort Wayne. "Not really," he said. "I just wanted to clarify things. I am reasonable. I am a bargain. But I am not cheap."

"You're also a very funny man."

"Funny ha-ha or funny strange?"

"I repeat, you are a rather sensitive fellow."

He let silence sit between them for several moments, letting his tires eat up the dark miles of the night that separated them from town.

"I thought that was what women wanted," he finally said. "I thought modern women liked sensitive men and that I was a true man of the eighties."

She appeared to be thinking for a moment. "I'd say we like them sensitive, but not thin-skinned."

"I see." He paused, squinting, until they'd passed a pickup going in the opposite direction. "And which am I?"

Ryan could feel Val's eyes on him. Her fingers danced lightly in the thicket of his hair. "Sensitive," she replied. "What else?" There was an electrical tension in the car. Val cleared her throat. "Do you have your hair permed like that?'' she asked. ''Or is it just naturally messy?''

''Everything about me is natural,'' he replied.

''That's good to know.'' She pulled her hand away, her voice appearing to be somewhat strained. Silence returned to sit between them.

The lights of the strip malls appeared on the horizon. It wouldn't be long before he dropped Val off and then went on to his own house, which would now seem ten times larger because of its emptiness. He let a small sigh escape.

''Miss your kids?''

Ryan clenched his jaw. Damn. Was she some kind of psychic or something, able to read his mind and look into the innermost corners of his soul?

''I could have driven up myself,'' she went on. ''That way you wouldn't have had to leave them until early tomorrow.''

''Next time we'll just plan on you staying overnight,'' he said. There was no reply and Ryan had a slight sinking feeling in his stomach. Would she resent him assuming that she'd want to stay over at the cottage? That she'd be free to join him on weekends?

''You could also work a three-or four-day week,'' she said. ''That way you could spend long weekends with your family.''

''No.'' He shook his head. ''We really need to get back to a more normal type of existence.'' Ryan paused at a flashing yellow light. ''Besides, my kids aren't the neediest ones around. I just got a request to develop a national awareness campaign for the Big Brother/Big Sister organization and those kids' problems really make my kids' seem small. My kids have only a single parent, but they have grandparents right here in town. They've lived in the same house and same stable neighborhood all their lives and now they have a very nice lady to care for them.''

Val didn't reply and Ryan glanced quickly at her out of the corner of his eye. Her face seemed quiet; she was just staring straight ahead. She was probably tired from the activities of the day, or had he awoken unpleasant memories of her own childhood?

''I guess I feel like there are other people more needy than my kids and if I have the chance to help them then I should,'' Ryan went on. ''I know I'm good at my work and that I can have a positive effect on the lives of a lot of people, so I guess I'm hoping my kids are willing to be generous.''

''You're a good man, Ryan Crawford.''

He was happy to see her smile, but he didn't want to sound like some pompous jerk. ''I do what I do because I enjoy it,'' he said.

''That's good,'' she replied. ''So do I.''

Her hand was lying on the seat by his side and Ryan let his hand drop over hers. They looked at a lot of things from the same perspective; the need to enjoy your job was just part of it. That's why they were able to become friends so quickly.

''Want to come in for a snack?'' Val asked. ''I've got some gourmet chocolate chip cookies and I pour a mean glass of milk.''

In the muted shadows of the parking lot lights it was difficult to see Ryan's reaction. Was he reading something else in her invitation or was he tired and interested only in going straight home? She wasn't exactly sure why she'd even asked him, except that now that the day was over she was perversely sorry to see it end.

"I've heard milk and cookies help all boys, big and little, get to sleep faster, but I can make coffee if you like," she said.

He moved to his door and she could see a smile on his face. "Milk and cookies will be fine. I was just trying to decide if it was better to face the empty house right away or delay it a little longer."

"And you opted for delay?" she asked as she opened her car door.

"I figured anything's easier to face with chocolate chips in your bloodstream."

He took her bag from the back despite her efforts to take it herself. He seemed so determined that the choice appeared to be between wrestling and letting him play the gentleman. The asphalt would be a little hard for tumbling about on, so Val opted to let Ryan play Sir Walter Raleigh.

The town house was silent and dark when she unlocked the door. The darkness was easily dispelled by switching on the lights, but the silence seemed more oppressive than normal. She stepped aside to let Ryan enter and two wheat-colored balls of fur with dark masks around their eyes came out of the kitchen to glare at her.

"Ah, the welcoming committee," Ryan said as he put her bag down. "Why is it they don't look pleased to see me? They have first dibs on the chocolate chip cookies?"

Val laughed and scooped up the two small cats. "This is Yin and Yang. They're Himalayans and look unfriendly, but they're really little sweethearts."

"Sure. That must be why they're licking their chops as they watch me."

She smiled at him. "Come on in the kitchen." She led him through the dining area and into her kitchen, which suddenly looked over-bright and efficient. Antiseptic almost, compared with the warm charm of Ryan's home.

"You and Casey were having quite a talk after dinner," Ryan said as he took a seat at the breakfast bar.

Actually it was an every-meal-bar since that was where she always ate. She entertained for business about once a month, sometimes on a large scale, sometimes a small, but most of her time here was spent alone. She changed the cats' water and refilled their dish of dry cereal, scolding herself away from a sudden attack of the mopes.

"Here are the cookies," she said brightly and opened the cookie jar for him, then poured two glasses of milk.

Ryan munched one cookie, then took another. "These are great. Did you bake them yourself?"

Val shook her head and set their glasses down as she sat on the other stool. "If I had, they wouldn't have come out this good."

"I thought you were a woman of many talents."

"Not baking. I don't have the patience for it." She drank some milk. "There's a little bakery around the corner from my office."

"The one with that funny French name? I've heard about them. I'll have to drop over there someday. The kids would love their stuff."

"Would you like any more?" she asked.

"No, thanks. Too many treats and I get fat." His eyes lingered on the cookies though, then he took another. "Little boys like chocolate chip the best of all," he said.

His eyes beamed at her over a boyish smile and Val felt a tightening around her heart. Her breathing became harder, forcing her to look away. She moved her glass in a small, careful circle, echoing the pattern of the countertop. What was there about his smile that she could feel down in her toes? She felt under seige, as if she had to keep watch all the time around him because she never knew when her foolish heart was going to go all soft and mushy on her. Time to switch to a safer topic.

"Casey was asking me to keep an eye on you when we were talking after dinner," she told him.

"An eye on me? She afraid I'll eat too many chocolate chip cookies?"

Val grinned, slightly embarrassed by Casey's worries, but still Ryan ought to know. "Well, actually, she's afraid some evil woman is going to get her clutches into you and steal you away from them."

The teasing light faded from his eyes. "I hope you told her that's not going to happen."

"I tried," Val said. "I think her real fear is being separated from you. It's not that long since her mother died and then to have you out of her sight for days at a time worries her. She's realized how fragile life is and feels you're all vulnerable."

"I've promised to call every evening and spend every weekend up there, so I hope that reassures her."

"Nothing will but time," Val said.

Ryan sighed and found her hand. "You sure got more than you bargained for when becoming friends with me."

His touch was warm, and sweet, silent music seemed to fill the air. This was where he should lean over and kiss her, this was where her heart should make her slip into his arms. But her mind was screaming out warnings louder than any whisperings her heart could make and she got to her feet, pulling her hand free.

"Would you like to see the rest of my home?" she asked, jumping up. Space and movement erased the wobblies from her legs.

"Sure."

He followed her back into the living room. Suddenly the sweeping cathedral ceiling and the balcony in front of the bedrooms looked even more sterile. "It doesn't have your home's Victorian charm," she said. "But it's functional and easy to care for."

Ryan looked around and nodded. "I don't think my place has ever looked this neat." He took another pass around the room. "Or ever will."

"I'm sure my cats are a lot easier on a house than kids."

"I don't think my kids would fit too well in here." There was a bemused smile on his face and Val knew he hadn't meant anything nasty, but the stab of pain in her heart almost made her cry out.

Would any child fit in her life? Maybe any kind of life was better for her son than even the best life she could have given him. Even given her present comfortable financial circumstances she probably still wouldn't make it as a mother. She didn't know how to relate to kids, how to make a home for one. How to make chocolate chip cookies. Why didn't she just leave well enough alone?

"Val?"

Blinking, she restored her focus and looked right into Ryan's concerned brown eyes.

"Is anything wrong?"

"No," she snapped. Denial kept the pain at bay at least for the moment. "Why should there be?"

"I don't know." He seemed taken aback. "It just looked like you were bothered about something."

Screaming at him that she was fine was not the thing to do. Certainly not for an executive with a reputation for cool capability. Val forced a smile to her face. "I probably just OD'd on fresh air and sunshine today."

"Yeah, that can happen."

"Well," she said brightly as she took a deep breath and then forcefully expelled it. "We both have busy days tomorrow."

"Throwing me out?"

"I wouldn't want to do that."

He stared at her so intently that Val had to look away. She found the fires of earnest concern burning in his eyes to be rather bothersome, but there was no way she was going to tell him about her son and the emptiness in her life because of his absence.

"Are you sure you're okay?"

She felt her hands engulfed in his. Forcing her smile still wider and keeping her eyes open wide, Val forced herself to look into the soft warmth of his eyes. "I'm fine. Nothing wrong with me that a full night's sleep won't cure."

"Okay."

His voice was soft like his eyes. His kiss, dancing on her lips, was equally soft. A softness that seemed to throb with a tension and a strength deep within it. Her heart wanted to cling to him, but she wouldn't let it.

"Get right to bed."

"I will."

She walked him to her door.

"Okay if I give you a call? If you're busy, I'll just leave a message. A polite message."

She smiled. He kissed her again and then was gone. Val collapsed back against the door and thanked the gods that he'd finally left. She didn't know how much longer she would have been able to maintain that brave front.

She slowly made her way back to the kitchen. She put the cookies away and washed out the milk glasses then turned off the lights and headed toward her bedroom, Yin and Yang following along behind her.

She took out her nightgown but suddenly didn't feel sleepy. Kicking off her shoes, she sat on the bed. Why couldn't she just leave the past alone? Her son was probably set in a life of his own now, a life that had no room for her. But what if he needed her? What if things weren't going well? Those two questions kept pounding on her. Was it her son calling her through some psychic phenomenon or was it just her guilt tearing at her?

She reached for the phone and dialed the detective's home number. A sleepy voice answered.

"I'm sorry to bother you," Val said. "But I was wondering if there were any new developments."

"Nope. I told you up front that these things are tough," he said. "They don't always succeed and even if they do, it takes time."

"I know and I'm sorry for bothering you."

"Don't worry about it," he laughed. "It's your money."

"Well, thank you for your patience."

"That's what we both need," he replied. "I'll keep plugging away. We'll get lucky one of these days and something will break. I guarantee it."

She took a deep breath. "Thank you."

"I'll keep in touch," he said. "And don't worry."

A pained smile twisted her lips. Translated that meant don't call me, I'll call you. After hanging up, Val stared at the wall. The weariness was increasing in her body, but it came with an extra measure of tension and pain. She had never felt so alone. It was going to be a long night.

Chapter Seven

Monday dawned, bright and sunny, but Val felt irritable all day. The challenges that arose at work were solvable, yet it was as if a little mouse nibbled away at her contentment until the whole world seemed dark and gloomy. When Ryan called and asked if she'd like to have dinner with him at the German Fest, she jumped at the invitation.

He met her after work in the lobby of her office building, his smile more potent than the sun. She felt the gloom slip off her shoulders. She'd isolated herself too much and for too long, she decided. Having someone to talk to, to confide in, made all the difference.

Together they walked down the street to the plazas where the fest was held each year. The scent of the German food reached out to greet them and her smile grew.

"You come to this before?" Val asked.

"Not for ages. My parents used to bring me and my brothers to it when we were kids. That was before I developed an appreciation of sauerkraut. We'd get very creative in trying to avoid it."

A beer garden had been set up around the fountain in the First National Bank plaza and they got in line to purchase their food. "I didn't know you had brothers," she said.

Ryan nodded. "There were four of us. I'm the only one left in the area besides Mom and Dad. Tom went into computers and gets transferred all over. He's in Los Angeles right now. Pat's a professor of mathematics over at the University of Ohio and Doug lives in the Chicago suburbs, selling insurance."

"Do you see much of them?"

"We try to get together at Christmas but it's hard. Tom's got a wife and four kids so it's expensive for them all to fly in. Pat and Doug can drive, but it's an investment of a couple of days at least. So some Christmases are more hectic than others."

None of Val's Christmases were hectic, hadn't been for years and years. She wouldn't mind having them mean something again, having a reason to decorate her home and her spirits. But it was their turn to order wiener schnitzel and dumplings, sauerkraut and bratwurst, and two frosted mugs of beer, so she was saved a reply. By the time they were sitting down at a table next to the fountain, the mood had changed and so would the topic.

"Hard day?" he asked.

She frowned her confusion. "Not really, why do you ask?"

"Just the look of pleasure on your face. I thought maybe it was the first time today that you got to relax.

Although now that you've got the Crawfords settled, you must be on easy street. No one could be as difficult as we were."

"Each job is a little bit different."

"Always diplomatic."

"That doesn't sound like a compliment."

"It's just a fact. You don't give much of anything away about yourself. I feel like I've had to pry everything I know about you out with a crowbar."

She took a bite of the bratwurst, chewing slowly and carefully as she played for time. "I've always been a private person," she said. "But I'm not as bad as you make me sound. I've talked about myself."

"Not much."

"I have too," she argued. "There just isn't that much to tell. I grew up in Houston, was orphaned at eleven, had a year of college and now own my own business. That's all there is."

His eyes glittered with a strange irritation and he reached across the table to take her hand in his. "Why do you put yourself down so much? There's a lot more to you than can be summed up in a few sentences. Is this what growing up in foster homes did to you?"

"Maybe." His questions were hitting too close to home. She tried to pull her hand free but he wouldn't let her. She picked up her beer with her other hand and took a sip. His eyes were watching her closely, then he gently released her hand and let her reclaim it. Inexplicably she felt cold and alone.

"Did they have the Big Sister program when you were a kid?" he asked.

"Sure." She took another drink of her beer, using both hands to hold the mug. They felt less empty when busy. "But there were about fifty kids for every adult volunteer."

"What about the families you lived with? Some of them must have taken an interest in you."

Val frowned, seeing back into a past that she chose to visit only on rare occasions. She played with her food, moving it from one side of her plate to the other side. "Most of them were good, kind people," she said slowly. "But they were overworked and weren't equipped to deal with the problems they faced. They fed and clothed me, kept a roof over my head, but developing a relationship with every kid they were given just would have taken more time and energy than they had. I didn't cause trouble so I was pretty much ignored."

"But time alone would help you build relationships."

"With whom?" she asked with a shrug. Her eyes moved to the fountain beside them. Lights on the bottom shone upwards so that a blanket of diamonds seemed to lie glittering just below the surface, just out of reach.

"Most of the families had been in the system a long time. They'd stopped believing they could make a difference. One woman wouldn't give me a house key even though I got home from school two hours before she got home from work because she didn't trust me. Oh, it wasn't me really. I guess she'd been burned before and didn't trust any foster kids she got, but it didn't make for the beginnings of a real relationship."

"That's awful."

She shook her head. "That's life."

"But it shouldn't be," he snapped.

She had to smile. He was the knight in shining armor coming to the rescue, except that he was about twenty years too late. Still, the burden of the past lifted a little.

"It's over and done with," she told him gently. "It's nice to know you care, but save your anger for things that can still be changed."

His eyes grew darker, taking on a more intent gaze as his hands found hers. "If there's anything I can do to make you feel better, just say so."

There was a tension in the air, a sparking of new energies that had been lying dormant for a long time. Her heart tried to devour him, reading a closeness in his gaze, in the touch of his hands, that wanted to bring tears to her eyes. She wanted to lie in his arms and rest in his strength. She wanted to let his gentleness consume her. Then her heart took a sudden turn toward sanity. She wanted to run.

Val wrapped her nervousness in light laughter. "It would make me feel terrifically good if I could finish my dinner."

The intensity of his eyes died down. "Sure."

He let go of her hands and they finished their meal in silence. Her racing heart returned to normal, just as preferred, she assured herself.

"Sounds like the folk dancing exhibition is about to start," he said, indicating the direction where the music was coming from with a nod of his head. "Want to go see it?"

"Fine with me," she replied. She hadn't intended to confide in him, and she certainly hadn't expected to feel so comfortable in doing so.

They disposed of their garbage and walked over to the next plaza, where a crowd was gathering. Rather than taking a seat in the bleachers, Ryan led her back toward the stairs that led down into the plaza.

"You can see better from up here," he said, leading her about three quarters of the way up.

Other couples, sharing their preference, were already seating themselves on the stairs and on a chest-high retaining wall. But they were unlike the other couples, in that Val kept her hands carefully in her lap and sat far enough from Ryan so as not to be seeming to expect him to put his arm around her shoulder. She didn't want him to think she was misinterpreting their relationship.

Below them, dancers and band members were dressed in ethnic costumes. The men in their lederhosen—leather shorts with suspenders—and the women in their brightly colored, vested, peasant dresses were dancing to lively, polkalike pieces. The music and the carefree abandon of the performances soon had Val feeling lighthearted. Was it so terrible to feel close to a friend? To share the hurts of the past so that they understood who you were and where you came from? She edged just a touch closer to Ryan as they applauded the end of the dance, then smiled as he took her hand to help her to her feet.

"I heard they're supposed to play slow stuff over by the government center," he said. "Want to go over and dance?"

"That would be very nice."

He didn't let go of her hand and this time she didn't object, not even in the deepest recesses of her heart. They walked down the street, letting the growing shadows of evening surround them as the soft, slow sounds of a waltz floated on the summer's evening breeze. Val felt comfortable.

"Miss the kids?"

"I guess." He fell silent and Val waited, feeling that he was going to say more. "It's hard to explain. After being married, with a family, for so many years, it feels very strange to be alone."

"You're not really alone," she said. "You have people at work."

"And I have you." He gave her a quick kiss and Val let the warm glow it gave her spread all the way to her toes.

"You know, maybe it's good for you and the kids to be separated a bit," she said. "Especially after you spent so much time with them over the past year or so."

"I agree. They need some time apart from me to grow. I'm just a little lonely sometimes."

She squeezed his hand and felt a momentary surprise when he let go of her. The surprise turned to sweetness as he put his arm around her shoulder and pulled her closer. It felt so good, so right, to be together. She could feel his heart beating and felt the fears and shadows of the past fade even further away, no longer able to touch her.

"It'll be fun to dance," she said. "I haven't done much of that lately."

"Neither have I."

"I heard that regular dancing is becoming popular again," Val said as they reached the plaza. The band was on a dais and small tables were scattered about close to the office buildings, while couples danced in the center.

"I guess people are just getting smarter. Dancing is the perfect excuse to hold a beautiful woman in your arms. That is, if this beautiful woman will do me the honor?" He released her, waving one hand toward the dancing couples.

She curtsied with a smile. "Thank you, sir, I believe I will."

Ryan took her in his arms and they moved with surprising ease into the measured steps of a waltz. Their feet stepped in unison, their hearts seemed to beat as one.

Caught up in the music, with its sweet rhythm and majesty, she seemed to be floating in the clouds. Ryan's arms held her securely, while their souls seemed to merge and sing. When the music ended, he kept his arms around her, bending to gently kiss her lips.

A niggling worry opened its eyes. "Is this all part of friendship?" she asked.

"Absolutely," he said, not moving his arms for a moment, then slowly letting them fall along with his smile. "Unless you—"

"No, no," she quickly assured him. "I've got no complaints. We're adults and closeness leads to closeness, but doesn't have to lead to commitment."

"Or to expectations."

She smiled up at him. "Well, I don't know about that. I certainly expect to have another dance with you."

His smile seemed to grow from deep inside him, warming her heart as it spread to his eyes. "Well for that matter, I commit myself to dancing with you all evening."

He took her once again in his arms, swaying with the music and with their own inner songs. Val looked up above her. Beyond the towering office buildings and past the reach of the dim lights around the dancing area, she could see the moon, golden and watchful. A lovers' moon, but it didn't scare her in the least because they weren't breaking any of their rules.

Wednesday evening was Humphrey Bogart night at an old-fashioned theatre near the river, and Val discovered with delight that Ryan was a great fan of the old movies, just as she was. They met after a longer than normal workday and watched *The African Queen*, holding hands and sharing a box of popcorn. When the movie was over, they stood for a moment under the marquee and stared up and down the empty streets.

"You hungry yet?" Ryan asked.

Val shrugged. "You?"

"So, so," he replied. "I ate a late lunch."

"Me too. Why don't we just walk around a bit?"

"It's going to rain," he said, pointing to the lightning in the distance.

"Aw," she teased. "Are you scared to get wet?"

Ryan just looked at her, his eyes full of warning and promise. A slight shiver tiptoed down her spine, a shiver that begged to expand into full-fledged hungers, but Val chose levity instead.

"I'm not afraid of the rain," she said, her voice louder than need be. "No sir, not me."

He didn't even blink and Val watched warning war with promise until warning left and promise became distant. "I was merely being a gentleman, concerned about your welfare," he said.

"Sorry," she said, surpressing a giggle.

"I see no reason for your abuse."

"I'm very sorry."

Warning came sneaking back in and Val swallowed her giggle. "Jeans, a cotton blouse and sneakers are hardly bothered by a little rain," she said. "Or even a lot of rain."

"I was thinking of your hair."

"It's waterproof," she pointed out.

His frown was lacking something in severity as he sighed and took her hand. "Then let's go for a walk," he growled.

"Yes, sir."

They walked in a companionable silence down toward the river, hand in hand like two...like two friends.

"A penny for your thoughts," Ryan said as they stopped to lean against the railing.

"You're going to have to do better than that," she said in a reasonable replica of a male growl. "I don't come that cheap. I'm very reasonable, but not cheap."

"I suppose you know why donkeys don't go to college?"

"Nobody likes a smart aleck."

Ryan put his arm around Val's waist and drew her closer. They watched the river flow by, the heavy about-to-rain silence broken only by the gentle lapping of water against the seawall. Life was about as perfect as it could get. A little flickering flame in her stomach questioned that thought, but Val ignored it.

"Where do you want to eat?" she asked.

"I don't care."

"What do you have a taste for?"

"Anything."

"Boy, can't you make a simple decision? What kind of an executive are you anyway?"

"The off duty kind," he said.

"I didn't know executives ever went off duty."

"This one does," he said. "No executive tie, no decisions."

"So in a T-shirt or no shirt, you can't make a decision."

"That's right."

"Now's a fine time to tell me," she grumbled.

They went back to watching the river in silence. Finally, at a break in the action, Ryan asked, "You're a business owner and executive, why don't you decide where we should eat?"

"Can't," she replied. "I'm off duty."

He gave her a "come on" look.

"Hey," she said. "You see my executive pumps?"

He shook his head.

"No leather pumps, no decisions," she said with finality in her voice. "We'll just have to let the gods decide."

"Okay."

They stared jointly down at the water swirling below them.

"How long do you think this will take?" Ryan asked.

Before Val could reply, there was an enormous crack of thunder, as if the gods themselves were answering. The wind increased and even in the darkness they could see the large, dark cloud bank that was directly overhead.

"It's going to pour." Even before all the words were out of his mouth, large drops were splattering down on them.

"It's going to be a gully washer." Val began running.

Ryan followed, overtaking her and taking her hand. "I think there's a little joint over back by the theatre."

They were soaked but soon came to the neighborhood bar in between a shoe repair shop and a consignment store for women's clothes. There was no canopy outside and they tumbled in, dripping onto the dark wood floor. Three men and a woman were sitting there.

The bartender looked up and smiled. "Hey, look what the storm washed up."

"It's pouring out there," Ryan said with a laugh as he shook the drops from his head. Val wiped at her face with her hands.

The woman got up from her stool. "Go sit in the corner," she said. "It's away from the air conditioner draft. I'll get some towels."

Val was about to assure her that they were fine but the heavyset woman, moving surprisingly fast, was already gone.

"You'd better sit down," the bartender said, coming around the corner of the bar. "When Reva gives an order she likes it followed."

As they reached the designated corner table, Reva was already bustling out from the back, thick towels piled in her arms. "Let me cover those chairs before you sit down," she said. "I don't care about them getting wet, but it's more comfortable sitting on something that soaks up the wet from you."

They murmured their thanks and each took a towel to wipe their faces and arms.

"What would you like to drink?" Ryan asked Val.

"You don't have to buy anything," the bartender protested. "You come in and dry off, but you don't have to buy something."

"I'd like a glass of Rhine wine, please," Val said, basking in the man's genuine friendliness.

"Burgundy, please," Ryan said.

"Hey, I mean it," the bartender said. "You really don't have to buy anything."

"It would be cruel to deny us one little drink," Ryan said. "We haven't even had dinner yet."

"George," Reva said. "Get them their drinks before they sue us for discrimination."

"Yes," Val laughingly agreed. "I think there's something in the city statutes about serving people, no matter how wet they are."

"And bring some peanuts," Reva called to George. "They probably want a little something to munch on."

"You're not going to make much money telling people they don't have to buy anything," Ryan said, making conversation with Reva as they waited for George to bring over their drinks.

"We pay the rent," Reva said. "And both George and I get a pension, so we don't need much extra."

"So this is almost a hobby?" Val asked.

"Something like that," George said, putting the glasses in front of them. "When we first retired, we didn't do nothing but argue all the time. Then we stumbled onto this place. Now I got friends visiting all day and Reva picks on the customers. By the end of the day she's tired out and easy to get along with."

"How come you're so chintzy with the peanuts?" Reva asked accusingly.

"They said they haven't had dinner yet," George explained. "I figured they don't want to spoil their appetites."

"That's for them to decide, not you."

"They might want to eat a big dinner."

"Actually we're not that hungry," Ryan said.

"Yes," Val agreed. "We'd just like something light." She and Ryan turned to look at a menu written on a chalkboard.

"That's just for lunch," George said. Then he turned to Reva. "We got anything left over?"

Reva shook her head. "We had a big lunch crowd today and Sam," she indicated the group at the bar with her head, "had the last of the Swiss steak."

"Do you have any sandwiches?" Val asked.

"I could make some," Reva said. "What would you like, turkey, ham, roast beef?"

"Anything," Ryan said, and Val nodded her agreement.

"How about I make you a sub?" Reva asked. They both nodded and she disappeared into the kitchen, after telling George to give them some more peanuts.

George had to draw some beer for his other customers so that by the time he was returning with another bowl of peanuts, Reva was coming out of the kitchen with their sandwiches. She glared briefly at the bowl but said nothing. Obviously George had passed muster this time.

"I got some potato salad and fresh vegetables," she said. "And some people don't like mayo, so I put everything on the side."

Val looked at the oblong dish, the sandwich piled high with meats, cheeses, lettuce, and tomato, ringed by a mound of potato salad and raw carrot sticks and celery, and suddenly felt comfortably hungry.

"Thank you," she said.

"If you want some dessert later," Reva said, "I got some German chocolate cake and strawberry pie."

"I'm not sure how much room I'll have after this," Ryan said with a laugh. "But we'll see."

The couple left them and they turned their attention to the sandwiches. Val looked on as Ryan put mustard on his. The friendly warmth of the place had burned off any chill the rain might have left in their clothes and she felt like she was basking under the summer sun. She'd forgotten how much life could hold outside of one's job.

The sandwiches and potato salad were filling but, on Reva's insistance, they found room for dessert. George brought a generous piece of pie for her and a more than generous piece of cake for Ryan.

"Holy catfish," Ryan exclaimed. "It's almost a sin to eat all that."

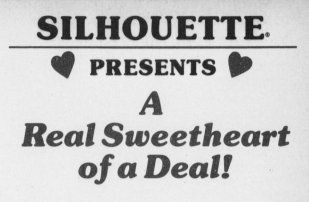

SILHOUETTE®

♥ PRESENTS ♥

A
Real Sweetheart
of a Deal!

**PEEL BACK THIS CARD AND SEE
WHAT YOU CAN GET! THEN...**

Complete the Hand Inside ➡

It's easy! To play your cards right,
just match this card
with the cards inside.
Turn over for more details...

Incredible, isn't it? Deal yourself in right now and get 6 fabulous gifts ABSOLUTELY FREE.

1. 4 BRAND NEW SILHOUETTE SPECIAL EDITION® NOVELS—FREE!

Sit back and enjoy the excitement, romance and thrills of four fantastic novels. You'll receive them as part of this winning streak!

2. A LOVELY BRACELET WATCH—FREE!

You'll love your elegant bracelet watch—this classic LCD quartz watch is a perfect expression of your style and good taste—and it's yours free as an added thanks for giving our Reader Service a try!

3. AN EXCITING MYSTERY BONUS—FREE!

And still your luck holds! You'll also receive a special mystery bonus. You'll be thrilled with this surprise gift. It will be the source of many compliments as well as a useful and attractive addition to your home.

PLUS

THERE'S MORE. THE DECK IS STACKED IN YOUR FAVOR. HERE ARE THREE MORE WINNING POINTS. YOU'LL ALSO RECEIVE:

4. FREE HOME DELIVERY

Imagine how you'll enjoy having the chance to preview the romantic adventures of our Silhouette heroines in the convenience of your own home! Here's how it works. Every month we'll deliver 6 new Silhouette Special Edition® novels right to your door. There's no obligation to buy, and if you decide to keep them, they'll be yours for only $2.74* each—that's a savings of 21¢ per book! And there's no charge for postage and handling—there are no hidden extras!

5. A MONTHLY NEWSLETTER—FREE!

It's our special "Silhouette" Newsletter—our members' privileged look at upcoming books and profiles of our most popular authors.

6. MORE GIFTS FROM TIME TO TIME—FREE!

It's easy to see why you have the winning hand. In addition to all the other special deals available only to our home subscribers, when you join the Silhouette Reader Service, you can look forward to additional free gifts throughout the year.

SO DEAL YOURSELF IN—YOU CAN'T HELP BUT WIN!

*In the future, prices and terms may change, but you always have the opportunity to cancel your subscription. Sales taxes applicable in N.Y. and Iowa.

Remember! To win this hand, all you have to do is place your sticker inside and DETACH AND MAIL THE CARD BELOW. You'll get four free books, a free bracelet watch and a mystery bonus.

BUT DON'T DELAY!
MAIL US YOUR LUCKY CARD TODAY!

BUSINESS REPLY CARD

First Class   Permit No. 717   Buffalo, NY

Postage will be paid by addressee

SILHOUETTE READER SERVICE™
901 Fuhrmann Blvd.
P.O. Box 1867
Buffalo, N.Y.
14240-9952

NO POSTAGE
NECESSARY
IF MAILED
IN THE
UNITED STATES

"That's okay," George replied. "It's a safe sin. Don't do nothing but put a few pounds on your waist and you can walk that off on your way home tonight."

He stood back and beamed as they each took their first bite. "Reva makes all the desserts herself."

"Delicious," Ryan said.

Val nodded her agreement.

"It's nice to get young couples like yourselves in here," George said. "You married?"

Val and Ryan looked at each other in surprise for a moment, then Val turned to the bartender. "We're just friends."

He smiled. "That's a good start." He moved on to refill someone's beer glass.

Val smiled at Ryan. "I guess he didn't understand."

"People get things like that confused," Ryan agreed. "You know, friendship and romance."

"Men and women can be friends, too."

They polished off the desserts, then paid their bill. After promising to return, they stepped out into the wet city streets. The rain had stopped, but the downpour had left everything smelling squeaky clean. Hand in hand, they walked back to Ryan's car before Ryan broke the silence.

"I told Mrs. Ricco she can have weekends off."

"Oh?"

"Want to come up to the cottage for the weekend with me? I wasn't planning an exciting Fourth of July, but maybe have a few sparklers, stuff like that."

There were enough sparks setting off between them lately, but Val didn't point that out.

"I could pick you up late Friday afternoon and bring you back Monday evening. Unless you can't leave the cats."

Val shook her head. "As long as they have lots of water and dry food, they're fine. I've been away for weekends before."

"We'd love to have you."

"I could take Casey shopping for her makeup," Val said.

"Yes," Ryan agreed. "She's anxious for you to do that."

"And I could help keep Robert from breaking more eggs."

"That would be real nice of you."

"Okay."

He leaned forward and kissed her, a lingering, promising touch that spoke of closeness and hungers, of the delight of peace after the storm. She moved into his arms, savoring the stillness around them. Old George was right. Friendship was a good place to start, but it didn't have to lead to marriage. It could just lead to a better friendship, a deeper friendship. A closer friendship.

Chapter Eight

Val heard soft footfalls coming behind her in the late evening's darkness. Then Ryan dropped himself onto the bench. Her heart welcomed his arrival. He was all she needed for the world to be perfect. The lake's gentle lapping at the pier, the stars overhead and a good friend at her side. She felt content and turned toward him.

"Casey throw you out?" Val asked.

"She pointed out that it was rather rude to leave a guest sitting all by herself."

Val chuckled.

"She said that she and the boys would clean up the dinner dishes and, if I was any kind of gentleman, I would see to it that you were properly entertained."

"Kid's getting tough in her old age."

"Tough to take." Val could sense him shaking his head. "If she were my sister I think I would be tempted to indulge in a bit of homicide."

"Hey, you want her to take charge," Val pointed out.

"She doesn't have to be so bossy about it."

Val chuckled again, slipped off her sneakers and ran her feet through the cool, damp grass. "Well, I'm ready."

"Ready for what?" he growled in question.

"Ready to be entertained." She snickered a little. "I mean if you're any kind of gentleman."

She could see his head turned toward her, but there wasn't enough light to see his eyes. If only she'd had a flashlight right now, she'd know what fueled the glow she presumed was in his eyes, warning or promise.

"Okay," he said slowly. "How about if I point out the various constellations and discuss them with you?"

"Be still my beating heart."

"If you don't like the idea, how about if I hold your head underwater and you can count the fish?"

"I love stars."

"Good choice."

He moved closer and put his arm around her shoulders. Her heartbeat sped. She leaned into him. There was a solidness, a strength about him. She could trust him not to break the rules and cause her pain.

"We'll start with the easiest first," he said. "There's the Big Dipper."

Val's eyes looked out to the heavens and lost whatever focus remained in them. The dark sky, dotted with stars and lit by a full moon, spread like an Arabian night's canopy over them. A gentle offshore breeze sent all the mosquitoes out over the lake, and Ryan's male scent, mixed in with his aftershave, filled all her senses. Their hearts beat in unison.

"And that's Sirius over there."

Her eyes followed his pointing hand, but her heart looked only to his. Her body leaned even closer into his, closer to the chiseled muscles of his chest. Her lips longed for his, breathed his name in the moon's own song and slowly found their way across the darkness that separated them. She touched his mouth with hers.

"Boo!"

It was two voices working as one and loud enough to cause both Val and Ryan to start.

"What the heck are you guys doing sneaking around like that?" Ryan snapped, spinning around to face the twins.

"Hi, guys," Val said with a voice full of resignation.

"I've got a good notion to send you two to bed," Ryan continued grumbling.

"They were just playing around," she said.

"Yeah, Dad, we were just playing around."

"Golly, where's your sense of humor?"

Val felt Ryan tense up next to her. "Your father was just startled," she told the boys. "He was thinking of something else."

"Next time we'll tell him before we sneak up on him," one twin said.

The other merely snickered and Ryan tensed up again. Val knew that she was going to have to come up with something to divert them or the twins would spend the weekend in their rooms with nothing to eat but liver and cauliflower.

"What did you guys do now?" Casey's voice carried authority with a comfortable ease.

"Nothing," one twin replied.

"Dad's being grumpy," the other added.

"Must mean you guys are cruisin' for a bruisin'," Casey said with a laugh.

"They're all having difficulties getting along," Val said. "Maybe we should separate them."

"I know," Casey said. "Let's play hide and seek."

"Flashlight hide and seek," the twins exclaimed in unison.

"Oh, goodie," Ryan grumbled.

Casey ignored him and spoke to Val. "The person who's it has the flashlight. And you're not found unless the light shines directly on you."

"The excitement is starting to get to me," Ryan said. "I'd better go inside and lie down."

"Oh, don't be such an old fuddy-duddy," Val chided him.

"Old?"

"I'll be it," Casey announced. "You guys hide while I go inside and get a flashlight."

"Fuddy-duddy?" Ryan's voice didn't sound at all friendly, but the swings in her feelings throughout the evening had left her giddy and she ignored his tone as she felt around the grass with her feet.

"What are you doing?"

"Looking for my shoes," she replied.

"We don't have time," he told her. "We have to hide before Casey comes back out."

"They're around here someplace."

"What are you?" he asked. "Some kind of wimp?"

A wimp? No one had ever called her a wimp before. "Let's go," she snapped.

He moved quickly toward the back of the property. At first Val stepped down hard on some large twigs, but she wasn't about to complain. She was no wimp and forced herself to concentrate, recalling the light-footed steps she'd used as a young child while running shoeless in the open fields around her home.

A shed loomed in the darkness and Ryan led her into some lilac bushes on the other side. "Aren't there some rules about staying on your property?" she asked.

"This is on the very edge," he said as he pulled her down to his side. "But it's still in our yard." Then, before she could settle down, he pulled her into his lap and wrapped his arms around her. "There are a couple of things I'd like to discuss while we have the time."

"Certainly." With his arms so tight around her, breathing was a bit difficult, but she didn't say anything about that. She wasn't a wimp.

"What sort of image do the words 'old' and 'fuddy-duddy' bring to mind?" he whispered, his hands running over her back lighting fires with his touch.

Val tried shrugging, but didn't quite make it. Her body seemed to be losing its independence, though she fought hard to keep her voice from betraying its weakness. "I don't know," she said. "A fuddy-duddy who happens to be old, I guess."

"And that's the picture I bring to mind?" Warning and promise that usually danced in his eyes had moved down into his voice. His hands had slipped lower, to glide along the curve of her leg while his lips danced along her neck.

"Sometimes," she whispered.

"Sometimes?"

"Not usually."

"But sometimes."

"Tonight. Just tonight." Her voice quickened and she seemed to be going backward. His lips came close to hers and her heart begged for their touch.

"Just tonight?"

Ryan whispered his question and she didn't quite hear her reply. His arms tightened even more, his lips on hers as her breath came in short gasps. What magic did he have in his touch, in his caress, that could awaken such fires in her soul? A flash of light blinded her.

"I see you guys," Casey said gleefully. "I've already found Richard. I just have to find Robert."

The flashlight went away and Val was left lying in Ryan's arms, the branch of a lilac bush scratching her arm. "What do we do now?" she asked.

Ryan first cleared his throat. "If I remember the rules correctly," he said, "when we're found we go back to where we started."

"Then I guess we'd better get there."

He gently slid her off him and scrambled to his feet, helping her up then. They walked slowly and silently back to the bench. Val's heart was heavy with the promise of desire and the emptiness the broken promise had left in its wake. There was a squeal of delight from over near the house as they neared the bench, where Richard was already sitting.

"I think she found Robert," Richard said.

"Casey's good at games," Val noted.

"Very," Ryan replied dryly.

Ryan came back into the kitchen after getting the boys to bed and found Val pouring herself a glass of iced tea.

"Can I pour you one?"

He nodded and sank onto a kitchen chair, trying not to watch her as she moved but finding it impossible not to. Her shorts and T-shirt did little to hide the curves of her body. She moved with grace and lightness. The fire began to smolder anew and he drank deeply of his iced tea.

"Sounds deathly quiet in there," Val said. "You didn't kill them, did you?" She sat down around the corner from him, tucking her bare feet under her.

"Did you ever find your sneakers?" he asked.

"I didn't look very hard," Val said, shrugging her shoulders. "I'll find them in the morning. Anyway, you never told me what you did with the children. You've got me worried now."

He felt the warmth of a soft smile move across his face. "The twins zonked out as soon as their heads hit the pillow. Casey's reading, but I'll bet she'll be in dreamland soon."

"I hope she's not a light sleeper," Val said. "I don't want to wake her when I go to bed."

Primeval urges that rivaled those of any teenage boy surged momentarily through his body. The easiest way not to disturb Casey was not to sleep in her room. There was more than enough room in his bedroom. Ryan sighed and stared down at his glass. "We need to talk."

Val nodded.

"Let's do it outside," he said. "The walls of these old cottages are rather thin."

She followed him out. They walked through the darkness down to the pier, seeing their way by the glow of an enormous moon. His hand ached to hold hers and it took an enormous amount of will to keep it down by his side, but he managed. There had already been enough hanky-panky this evening.

"Nice breeze," Val said.

"Real nice," Ryan laughed. "It'll give all our mosquitoes to our neighbors across the lake."

He slipped off his own sneakers, tossing them onto the grass, and led her to the end of the wooden pier. The wood was still warm from the day's sun and still slightly damp from the splashing antics of the kids. He and Val both sat down, letting their feet dangle in the water. The silence and the quiet star-studded sky wrapped a blanket of cool comfort around their shoulders. Ryan took Val's hand in his.

"Casey is a very cool young lady," Val said.

Ryan grunted affirmatively.

"I don't think she even blinked when she shined that flashlight on us. She just went on with the game."

"I think she was too surprised to do anything else," Ryan said.

"Could be."

They fell back into silence again, broken only by occasional splashing as their feet moved, slowly and gently, back and forth in the water. Crickets chirped in the nearby darkness and fireflies sparkled here and there across the lake. The urges within him had cooled now and what was left was a warm and easy comfort. Val was a nice lady to be with. He let go of her hand and put his arm around her shoulder.

"It all happened so fast," Ryan said. "I think if we just play it cool, Casey won't think anything of it."

"I don't think she's dumb," Val laughed.

"I'm not saying she's dumb. But it was dark and in the momentary glare of a flashlight, I'm sure she's not really certain of what she saw."

"I agree that we shouldn't make a big deal of it," Val said.

"Right," Ryan said. "The kids would have a hard time understanding it."

"A beautiful summer's night and two good friends."

"Dangerous combination," Ryan said.

"Absolutely," Val agreed.

They tried taking refuge in the silence again. But it was a noisy silence, the silence of a midsummer's night bellowing with the vitality and passions of life. Frogs croaked out their poems, thousands of unknown insects whispered their sonnets, and the reeds rustled as little creatures slithered and crept to secret meetings. Wonderful. What he really needed was a cold shower.

"We'd better play it cool while we're here," Ryan said.

"I agree," Val said. "The children would find it difficult to understand that we're just friends. That adults sometimes have needs that have nothing to do with emotions."

"They'd think it was more than that."

Val turned slightly under his arm and touched his chest lightly. His heart raced, but he forced his arm to retain its gentle hold on her.

"I'd never want to do anything that would upset your kids," she told him. "They've been through enough without having to worry about my place in your life."

His free hand came up to touch her shoulder, to run lightly down her bare arm. Her skin was so soft, so cool to his touch when he felt all afire.

"I appreciate that. Maybe that's why I feel so comfortable with you."

"And I hope your kids realize that too. Maybe I should have a little talk with Casey."

Ryan's hold on her shoulders tightened, his lips brushed her hair. "It's really nice to have a friend like you," he said. "I sure would hate to lose that."

"You won't," she promised. "We'll make sure your kids aren't threatened by me and we'll go on having fun together."

They were close and by leaning just a little closer they'd be able to kiss. They did just that. The fire flared into wild hungers. He wanted to hold her closer and closer, to spend the night in her embrace, but now was neither the time nor the place to let passions get the better of him. He pulled back regretfully.

"We should probably go in. I don't want Casey to get up and come looking for us."

"Well then, we'd better get in fast." Val giggled. "I don't think I can handle another session in the glare of that flashlight."

He stood up and helped Val to her feet. Then somehow she was in his arms again. His lips touched hers, his hands raced over her back, pressing her soft warmth into him. Dreams danced through his mind, but he pushed them aside and put her gently away from him.

"Just a little something to tide me over," he said with a shaking attempt at a laugh.

Val just took his hand and they walked back up the lawn toward the house. "Are you going to look for your shoes?"

"I'll get them in the morning," he said. Another few moments out here in the darkness with her and they might not part until morning. He was a father, he reminded himself, and that had to come first. But he was looking forward to that cold shower.

Val hardly slept the whole night, then dozed off around dawn only to dream of Ryan's arms holding her, of his lips waking wild passions in her. Not certain that she could maintain her distance as they had decided, she stayed in bed late, then took a long shower until Ryan had to be occupied somewhere else with the kids. She glanced out the window. As she dried herself off, she saw

Ryan and the twins putting the small sailboat out onto the lake. Casey wasn't with them. Maybe she'd gone out to visit one of her friends. Val hurried down to the room she shared with Casey and got dressed. A soft tap on the door told Val that the girl wasn't visiting anyone.

"Come in," Val said softly.

"Hi." Casey peeked around the door, then tentatively came into the room. "Are you all right?"

"I'm fine," Val assured her, trying to put a depth of assurance in her voice. "Why do you ask?"

"I wasn't sure that you'd slept all that well," Casey replied.

Had the girl noticed her tossing and turning all night? She tried to be as quiet as possible and after a few tries Val thought she'd found the silent spot in the springs.

"Did I keep you awake?"

"Oh, no," Casey assured her. "It's just that I heard you talking in your sleep a few times."

Val swallowed the lump of dread that rose in her throat. She hadn't thought she'd slept long enough at any given stretch to talk.

"What did I say?" Val asked, not certain she wanted to know.

"Oh, I couldn't make out the words," Casey said. "You were mostly mumbling."

Thank God for small favors. "I'm relieved," Val said with a laugh. "I was hoping that my secrets would be safe."

Casey moved to her bed and slouched back on it, the beautiful combination of ungainly and graceful that was a thirteen-year-old girl. Bright blue eyes, filled with that unique mixture of innocent child and worldly-wise woman, fixed their level gaze on Val. She quickly put her shoes on, avoiding that look.

"You slept late today," Casey said.

Val concentrated for a long moment on tying her shoes just right. "I guess I must have been tired."

"Too much fun and games last night, huh?"

Val looked up sharply at the girl, but those baby blues were still open wide, shining forth with that very special innocence of childhood. Val decided that Casey wasn't being a smart aleck. "Yeah, and it's so peaceful out here and quiet. Your nerves just sort of let go and you flake out."

Casey nodded. "It must be hard running a business of your own."

"It's a little tense at times," Val admitted. "But I enjoy it."

"Dad kept waiting for you to get up."

"Oh I'm sorry," Val said. "I hope that I wasn't keeping him from anything."

"He and the twins wanted you to go sailing with them."

"Why didn't you go with them?" Val asked Casey.

The girl threw her arms back and stretched. "We're together all week," she said. "I think it's good for siblings to be separate at times, don't you? And Dad and the boys should do man things together."

"True," Val murmured. "Exactly what I thought." That was as good an excuse as any she'd been able to come up with. Actually, it was better. She hadn't come up with any excuses this morning. All she could think of was Ryan and his arms around her, the taste of his lips and the hungers in her. If she had been able to think of excuses, she wouldn't have had to hide in bed this late and stay in the shower until she'd either worn off all her skin or looked like a prune.

Val looked across at Casey, trying to read what lay behind the girl's smiling eyes. They needed to talk. "Why don't we girls go out for lunch and shopping?" Val asked. "We can look at makeup while we're out, too."

"Okay," Casey exclaimed as she sprang out of bed. "That would be fun."

"We can take the whole afternoon off," Val said. "We'll leave a note for your dad saying not to expect us until dinnertime."

"Good," Casey replied. "They'll just goof off the rest of the day anyway."

They went to Kendallville where they found a nice restaurant for lunch, then a marvelous shopping center where they whiled away the afternoon. She and Casey had such a good time that it gave them enough material to keep the twins and Ryan entertained through dinner and into the evening. But once the boys were in bed, it was Val's turn to seek Ryan out.

"I talked to Casey today," she told him as they cleaned up the last of the dishes.

"Oh?" Worry crossed his eyes and she smiled her reassurance, but then the sound of the girl moving about in her room made Val glance over her shoulder.

"Want to go outside?" she asked.

He nodded and in a moment they were walking down to the lake, their feet bare and their hands clasped.

"The boys were hoping you'd go sailing with us," Ryan said.

"I didn't dare." The safe darkness gave her courage. "I thought the boys might be a bit surprised if I jumped on your bones."

He moved a bit closer, his arm going around her shoulders. "And was that a danger?" he asked, his lips brushing her hair lightly.

She pressed even nearer to him. "A distinct danger," she agreed. "I've been a bit unsettled since becoming your friend."

"Welcome to the club."

His voice was a whisper as he stopped walking to turn her toward him. His lips came down on hers and the night seemed alight with sparklers and Roman candles. Magic was in the air, sweet, wonderful magic. They pulled apart when breathing became a necessity and walked the few feet more to the end of the pier. They sat on the edge and let the summer's night surround them.

"So what did you and Casey talk about besides makeup?" he asked. "She didn't seem upset at dinner."

"She wasn't upset during the day, either." Val leaned against him, feeling his heart beat and wishing she were closer still. "I told her how we were friends and didn't want her to misunderstand our relationship.

"She said she and the boys liked me and that you seemed happier lately too."

"Oh, really?" Ryan pretended to take offense, but his hands were sliding down her arms, finding ways to keep her almost too close to him to breathe. "That wouldn't be due to finding a good housekeeper, now would it?"

Val let her lips find his in the darkness, not a difficult task at all, suddenly, and brushed them just enough to let the sweet fire of his touch ignite in her soul. "Now you and I know what's behind your sudden relaxed state, but Casey felt it was because you've got me for a friend."

"Funny you should mention relaxed," he said, breathing fire into her heart. "Relaxed is about as far from what I'm feeling as can be."

"I wasn't about to contradict her," Val said. "Then she might have guessed why I was avoiding you."

His hands roamed over her back, sliding under her shirt to bring the fire of his touch to her skin. "Are you going to avoid me again tomorrow?" he asked.

"Most likely," she whispered back, her voice a moan of desire. "I've never been good at pretending."

"Maybe we'll have to do something about it once we get back to the city."

"That sounds like a good idea," Val said. She slowly pulled her hands from his body, lying against him only long enough to steel her will. "We ought to go in."

His hands showed their reluctance to leave her but did, and he got to his feet. "Friendship is a lot harder than I thought."

"Are you two mad at each other?"

Val forced her attention back to the round dining table in the eating alcove off the kitchen. Sunday had passed with admirable restraint on both her part and Ryan's, ending with a trip to town to view some Fourth of July fireworks that Val thought she and Ryan could easily surpass. Now it was Monday evening and a light rain was falling, a gentle and warm drizzle, not enough to dampen most outdoor activities, but enough to force them inside for dinner. Ryan had put together a simple but substantial meal of grilled steak and baked potatoes.

Val sighed. Casey had voiced the question, but the boys' anxious faces carried the same load of concern.

"No," Val replied. "We aren't mad at each other. Not at all."

"Well, you two haven't said two words to each other all through dinner."

She and Ryan exchanged glances. Were they that obvious? They had concentrated so hard on being normal that they had turned abnormal.

"If *we* acted this way," Robert said, "you'd say we were pouting."

"Yeah," Richard agreed. "You'd probably send us to bed."

Ryan's eyes met hers for a brief, flashing moment before looking away. It was obvious that he didn't view an early bedtime as quite the same punishment Richard did, but Ryan tried to smile. "Hey, I'm sorry, guys," he said. "I guess we're just both thinking about the upcoming week. You know, our businesses and stuff," he ended lamely.

Val stared at Ryan for a moment. Brilliant. The man was absolutely brilliant. It was a wonderful excuse that the kids would buy.

"We're already planning what we will be doing tomorrow," she said quickly.

"That's right," Ryan agreed. "Got to get the week off to a good start or we won't accomplish anything."

Three pairs of eyes looked from one to the other. Disbelief was ripe in their gazes. "Still looks like pouting," Richard grumbled.

"You haven't really talked that much to each other the last couple of days," Robert added.

Ryan stared at her. The ball was in her court. "A lot of that was my fault," she said. "First, on Saturday I overslept."

"Then we went out to lunch," Casey said.

Val felt an overwhelming torrent of gratitude toward the girl. "Yes, it was a very nice lunch."

"How come you didn't take us?" Robert asked.

"You weren't here," Casey replied.

Twin glares burned at her. "And you wouldn't have liked it anyway," Val said. "It was a tearoom. A place where women like to eat." When they both made faces, Val knew that they had bought it. "And then we went shopping."

"You didn't buy anything," Richard said, accusation coming to reside in his face again.

"We bought makeup for me," Casey replied. "Just because I didn't show it to you doesn't mean we didn't get anything."

"Dumb makeup," Richard said. "Who'd want to see it anyway?"

"And then yesterday we were all busy celebrating the Fourth of July," Val said. "Who does much talking when you're watching parades and fireworks?"

The twins looked ready to argue, but Ryan got to his feet. "Let's clean up, guys," he ordered. Then as the children started clearing the table, he glanced out the window. Val thought she'd heard a car and Ryan confirmed it. "Mrs. Ricco is here."

The children rushed out to greet the housekeeper while Val and Ryan sat in silence for a moment, avoiding each other's eyes. The tension in the room grew so that she could almost see it, almost taste it.

"I should get my stuff together," Val said.

She hurried up to her room, eager hands throwing her dirty clothes and toothpaste into her overnight bag. Then there was nothing to do but leave. Mrs. Ricco insisted that they didn't have to go so soon, but the kids were engrossed in some summer evening variety show and didn't seem to care one way or the other. Both Val and Ryan made excuses about work they had to review before Monday.

The ride home was silent, the hungers growing with each passing mile. Val's heart raced with the motor. Her hand moved and suddenly found Ryan's.

"It was a nice weekend," she said as he pulled his car into her parking lot. They sat there a long moment. Val wasn't certain how to make the first move or even whether she should. What if Ryan had changed his mind?

"Would you like to come up for a drink?" she asked.

"Sure," he replied. He took her bag and followed her into her home. "Take care of your babies," he said, and went farther on in.

Val opened a can of food for Yin and Yang, added some to their dry food, then cleaned their boxes. After washing her hands, she cleaned up their dishes. Ryan still had not come in. She slipped off her shoes and slowly made her way up through the town house. Had he gone? Her stomach was twisted into knots.

Ryan was stretched out on her bed, his arms flung wide and his eyes closed. She stopped in the doorway and smiled, her heart about ready to burst with pleasure, but he didn't move. She took a step closer.

"Who's that sleeping in Goldilocks's bed?" she said gruffly. "Is it Papa Bear, Mama Bear or Baby Bear?" Ryan opened his eyes just as she pounced on the bed next to him.

"Baby Bear?" he growled at her. "Hey, lady, if you think I'm a Baby Bear, you need a little lesson in anatomy. I'm Papa Bear." He pulled her down onto the surface of the bed, next to him.

"Oh, are you?" she asked. "Well, Papa Bear, maybe you can help me. I came in with this very nice gentleman and I seem to have lost him."

He rolled over to pin her down on the bed beneath him. Her heart skipped a beat or maybe was just racing too fast for beats to be counted. She stared up into his eyes that glittered with a strange and fiery glow.

"You've been reading too many children's stories," Ryan said as his lips came down on hers.

The night seemed alive with song all of a sudden. Sweet magic melodies floated in the air to sweep her up into a dance of passion. Fires raged in the distance, lighting the darkness and spreading their warmth to her toes, to her fingers and slowly along her skin. His lips moved and tugged at hers, hungers calling her by name and waiting for her embrace.

His lips left hers even as his hands slid down her arms, waking every inch of her body to consuming desires. "You know there wasn't any porridge in the real version of Goldilocks," he said.

"Oh no?" Her voice was a weak whisper, a strained tremor that echoed the shaky state of her heart.

"And there was only one bear," he went on. His hands had gone exploring beyond her arms, under her shirt, to softer, more sensitive skin that was soon all afire.

"And what did this one bear do?" she asked. "Did he yell at Goldilocks for sitting in his chair?"

Val ran her fingers through his hair even as she spoke. How long had she wanted to do that? How long had these desires smoldered beneath the surface to flare up in such strength?

"Nope. He didn't care about any silly chair." Ryan's words were punctuated with tiny, breathless kisses that he placed along her neck.

"What about his bed then?" Val asked. Her hands cupped his face, reveling in the rough feel of his cheeks, in the freedom to touch and explore what she'd told herself was off-limits just days before. "Did he get mad at Goldilocks for lying in his bed?"

Ryan's smile was a spark to the kindling of her heart. Something in it touched and ignited the fiber of her being. "No," he said softly. "He'd been watching her for weeks, wanting her more and more every time he saw her but, you see, bears and beautiful young ladies aren't supposed to be good friends so he kept his hungers hidden."

"Until he ate her gentleman friend," Val finished for him.

Ryan pretended to frown. "Just the gentle part, until he could convince Goldilocks that she needn't fear him, that he just wanted to be her very, very good friend and that he'd never let her be hurt."

"And did she believe him?" Val asked.

But Ryan's hands had stopped. "I don't know," he said carefully. "Did she believe him? Did she trust that this wasn't just hormones or lust, but caring about a friend and wanting to share that care with her?"

Val touched his face gently, her hands speaking words from her heart. She smiled into his eyes, into his heart, she hoped, then let her hands slide down lower. Over his muscular chest and to his waist where a belt provided an easily unbuckled obstacle.

The flame in his eyes grew hotter, threatening to burn and scorch, but she wasn't afraid. This was like nothing that had ever happened to her before. She knew why he liked her, why they were friends, and that was the basis of their desire. She wasn't beholden to him, and he wasn't to her. They were equals in their hunger, equals in their trust.

"Yes, she believed him," Val said softly. "She knew that she could trust him."

Hungers were unleashed then, passions were aroused. Ryan undressed her, slowly, with almost a reverence, which made her impatience grow and her needs multiply. He pulled off her shirt and her bra, so that his hands could touch and explore her breasts. He caressed their softness, let his lips taste their sweetness, until Val felt ready to explode.

His chest was bare before her, a field for her hands to roam and delight in. The muscles were hard beneath the skin, but she could feel his heart beating so fast, as fast as her own. Her hands slipped around his waist and down below the tops of his shorts, pulling him closer to her hungers.

"Oh, Val," he said on a sigh. "Do you know what you're doing to me?"

"Trusting you?" she whispered as her lips burned a trail down his chest. "Befriending you?"

His movements grew more feverish, more impatient. Her shorts were tossed to the floor. He touched her, his hands roamed every inch of her, bringing to life depths that she'd thought were dead.

Then suddenly the fires could be held no more. He came to her and they were one. One heart beating out life's rhythms. One breath singing of ecstasy. One moment, suspended in time and for all eternity. She clung to him as the earth trembled and the stars stood still. Then slowly darkness swallowed her. Peace reigned over her and gentle sleep took her, still wrapped in Ryan's arms.

There never had been a moment like this before in her life and there never would be again, she thought. Her arms entwined around his heart and she drifted off to slumber. The gods had been kind to give her such a splendid glimpse of paradise.

Chapter Nine

Raindrops were hitting his eyelids. A soft, gentle summer rain, so warm and dry. *Dry?*

Ryan blinked and struggled to open his eyes. His vision was blurred, but it was good enough to see a little scowling face staring at him. A soft, furry face with a black mask and pushed-in nose. His vision slowly cleared and he saw another fuzzy body, wheat-colored, with the same black mask and pushed-in nose, leaning against Val's thigh and, like its partner, glaring with disapproval at him.

"Sorry, guys," he mumbled.

The cats continued glaring.

"She asked me to stay."

The cat nearest him flicked a tail, while the one leaning against Val coolly licked its paw. This was a tough interrogation team. *I wonder which one plays good cop* and which one bad cop? he thought. In reality, both sets of glaring eyes looked equally merciless.

"Okay," he said, still keeping his voice at a murmur. "So she didn't really ask me to stay. It . . . it just sort of worked out that way."

Both flicked their tails and were gone, twin wheaten blurs, streaking across the green carpet. Had he passed their test or would they be back, bringing a Bengal tiger with them? He plumped the pillow and made himself comfortable as he stared at Val sleeping peacefully, her face relaxed in a baby's soft vulnerability. It was obvious that she was in a land without fear and tension, so he didn't wake her, but looked around the room.

Everything here was earth tones—rust, browns, greens. The bedspread, cast so carelessly onto the floor, was a velvet quilt made of wide squares in varying shades of brown. The rug was a deep forest green, while the drapes were rust with streaks of gold where the morning sun tried to stream through. It was all soothing and relaxing, especially after the tension of the weekend.

Ryan closed his eyes. The last few days up at the lake had been fun, but he hadn't really relaxed. Everything seemed to pull him toward Val. If it wasn't her presence calling to his senses, it was her absence, making him ache for her. He wasn't surprised that their awareness of each other had exploded into passion last night, but what did surprise him was that the magic hadn't ended. Rather than part with awkward good-nights or even with smooth phrases, they'd fallen asleep in each other's arms, their bodies still entwined. Sometime around two in the morning, Val had stirred, wakening Ryan. She'd turned in her sleep, finding another position though not awakening herself. He could have left then, he supposed. Had he not wanted to sneak out like a thief in the night? Was the sound of Val's breathing, so comforting and so near; what had lulled him back to sleep? He hadn't stirred again until called by his feline interrogators.

Ryan felt Val start to waken, pulling the blanket a little tighter around herself as soft moans escaped her lips. Slowly she opened her eyes and blinked, then opened them wider. A crooked smile curved her lips.

"Hi," she whispered.

"Good morning," he murmured.

Suddenly her eyes opened all the way and she sat bolt upright in bed. "Ryan!"

"In the flesh," he replied.

Val's eyes stayed wide like a frightened deer's, her lips and cheeks twitching as she glanced quickly around her. "I forgot—" A quick swallow. "I didn't expect—" She took a deep breath. "What time is it?"

Ryan turned to look at the clock. "Almost seven-thirty. We have time for breakfast before work," he said. "Want to stop at the pancake house?"

She held the sheet high and tightly around herself. "No, I have to get to the office."

"You have a meeting?"

Val shook her. "No. I'm just never late."

"Rank should have its privileges," he said. "Otherwise why be boss?"

"I have to take a shower," she said, still clutching the sheet around herself. Val sat that way for several moments when it seemed to dawn on her that they'd already seen what there was to see of each other. Clenching her jaw, she let go of the sheets and slipped out of bed, giving him a tantalizing view of her firm breasts and gently curved bottom as she fled into the bathroom. She peeked back around the door a moment later.

"I'm sorry," she said. "I'm being a poor hostess. Would you like to shower first?"

"No," he said. "I'll do it at my place. I have to change for the office anyway."

Her pretty head disappeared and Ryan sat up in bed. It was obvious that Val was embarrassed. Or was it more than that? They had talked a lot about being friends, about not getting into an emotional relationship. She could very well be concerned about how last night would change their friendship.

The sound of water beating on a shower curtain stopped after a few moments and Ryan began marshaling his thoughts. They were good friends, but last night didn't have to change that. Neither of them wanted any kind of heavy relationship, but heavy referred to the emotions involved, not anything else.

Val stepped out of the bathroom, a towel wrapped around her body and her hair framing her face in wet ringlets. She moved quickly across the room and into her walk-in closet.

"I guess we were both rather tired yesterday," she called out.

Not that tired, Ryan thought as a smile seized his face. "I guess," he replied.

There were several minutes of silence and then Val stepped out in slacks and a white blouse, towel-drying her hair. "I'm not sure we should see each other for a while."

Ryan clenched his jaw for a moment. Damn it. There was nothing for her to be afraid of.

"I hope you're not letting last night interfere with a good frendship," he said.

She moved to her dresser, taking the long way around so they wouldn't get too close, and began to apply her makeup. "Things got out of hand."

He sought to calm the jitters in her voice. "We're not that old, and you're darn attractive."

His heart warmed at her smile, at the worries fading from her eyes. "You're not too bad-looking yourself."

"So our actions were not that unusual, given the circumstances."

Pausing with her makeup, Val turned from the mirror and faced Ryan directly. "Maybe our hormones shouldn't see each other for a while."

"Val, I don't think—"

The nervousness was back in her eyes. "I really have to get to work," she said quickly. "I have schedules and assignments that have to be taken care of in the beginning of the week and things are already out of whack because of the holiday yesterday."

Ryan slipped out of bed and reached for his pants, then went into the bathroom. Now wasn't the time for talking, that was obvious. He'd have to wait until she calmed down, until she saw that nothing in her life would change. By the time he came out, Val had dried her hair and was waiting at the bedroom door.

"Val," Ryan called as he picked up his shirt and pulled it over his head. "We need to talk this over. We're good friends and I can't see why we can't stay good friends."

"Ryan, I'm already late."

"Promise we'll talk things out."

"Ryan, I don't have time." She edged close to the door.

"Tonight."

"I don't know what my schedule is."

The panic in her tone worried him and he took a deep breath, willing calm into his voice. "Seven o'clock. If that's a problem, call me."

"Today's going to be hectic for me," she said. "I can't see myself being up to going out."

"I'll be here at seven," he said. "With pizza and wine."

Val was shaking her head. "Ryan, I—"

"I know," he said smiling. "You're already late. Go ahead. I'll lock up."

She gave him a look that would melt diamonds, then hurried downstairs.

"See you at seven," he called out.

A slamming door was his only reply. Ryan shook his head. He needed to convince her that last night didn't change a thing.

"Val, watch it," Marcie called out.

A hand bumped her shoulder and Val dropped the papers she was carrying. "Damn," she muttered. "We really have to put this copier someplace else."

"I told you I'd make the copies," her secretary scolded as she closed the drawer to the file cabinet.

"I know, I know." Val bent to pick up the scattered papers. "But I just needed a few things copied and you were busy." Besides, she needed activity to keep her mind occupied.

"Careful," Marcie said as she guided Val around the cabinet. "Don't knock something else down."

"I'm not helpless, you know."

"I never said you were," the secretary said. "You just seem a little out of it this morning."

Val began putting the papers back in order. She was more than a little out of it, she thought, and it wasn't just this morning. She must have been insane the whole weekend to let Ryan Crawford affect her that way.

"You still having problems with that Crawford family?"

Val dropped half the papers again. "What?"

Marcie bent down to pick them up, then handed them to Val. "I mean," she said with slow patience. "Did the latest housekeeper take off or something?"

"No," Val answered. "Mrs. Ricco is doing just fine."

"Good. You sure spent a lot of time on them."

"Well, that's probably all over now." Val straightened the papers and strode into her office.

"Next time let me do the copying," Marcie called after her.

Val left her with a wave and a smile, which she dropped as soon as the door had closed behind her. Marcie was right. Val had spent a lot of time on the Crawford family, but that was going to change. The Crawford family was in good shape now, and there was no need for any more of her personal attention. Her stomach did a few mild flip-flops. And there was no reason for her to have dinner with Ryan tonight.

Actually it wasn't really a dinner, one part of her mind corrected. It was pizza and wine, more of a snack than anything. Nothing at all to worry over. A couple of bites and he'd be leaving, which would be fine, another part added. She'd probably need to take some work to do at home tonight anyway. Things seemed to be running behind today.

Come to think of it, she ought to stay at the office tonight and catch up on her work. She never got much work done at home. She always forgot something and either had to go back to the office or just leave everything until the next day. Yes, staying late tonight would be best for everyone concerned, especially for herself. She'd put a call in to Ryan.

But a little voice wasn't sure about that idea. Wouldn't that be like running away? After all, she and Ryan were friends. They shared a number of interests. Her cheeks warmed at the idea of all they'd shared, and Val frowned. They'd made love, and didn't that mean they couldn't be friends anymore? Or could they?

Be honest, Val scolded herself. The real problem was her own reaction to last night, not Ryan's. It had felt too good to be there with him, to lie in his arms and feel so safe and secure. Her heart had been touched in a way that it hadn't been for years, in a way she'd vowed it never would be again. She couldn't let herself weaken, she couldn't soften and start looking for happily-ever-afters. They didn't exist, and she'd only end up hurt again.

Ryan had been open about his feelings. He knew the pain of love and wasn't going to suffer through it again. If he could be strong, then so could she. She just had to keep reminding herself of love's destructive power.

Sighing, Val returned to the work in front of her. It really had been sneaky of Ryan to set their dinner date at her house. That way she'd have to show up.

Though she supposed there were ways to get around that. She could stay in her office all night or get a motel room. Or take a trip out of town. Val pictured a forlorn Ryan sitting on the front steps with his pizza and wine until someone called the police. That would be cruel. She couldn't do that to a friend.

Come on, that part of her mind mocked, who was she fooling? He wouldn't sit on those front steps for long at all. There was a hoard of single women in the complex alone who would come along and take him in. Val frowned at the protest her heart made.

"Oh, hell!" she exclaimed. If she kept up this waffling all day, she'd have to stay in the office and work overnight just to do the work she was supposed to be doing right now. Calling on all the discipline she'd built up over the years, Val forced her attention to the administrative paperwork awaiting her attention.

The intercom buzzed and Val snatched it up as if it was the cause of all her problems. "Yes?"

"There's a call for you," Marcie said. "A Ross Chambliss and he said it's urgent."

Suddenly Val's hand on the receiver began to shake and her stomach twisted into a tight, painful knot. It was the private detective. Had he found out something about her son?

"Thanks, Marcie." Her voice was quivering and she swallowed hard. "I'll take care of it."

Ross Chambliss's voice came on the line. "Miss Dennison. Just wanted to let you know that I have a lead. The best one yet."

Val nodded, then realized he couldn't see her. "Oh?"

"I'm flying down to Fort Worth and I'll call if anything comes of it. Don't get your hopes up too high. A lot of these leads turn out to be dead ends."

"I understand that."

"Good," he said. "I'll be in touch as soon as I can, either way."

"Thank you," she said, but the dial tone was his only reply. A still shaking hand put the receiver in its hook. Val stared off into space for a long, long time.

Was she getting closer? Chambliss had warned her when he started looking that most of his leads turned out to be fruitless, but what if this one wasn't?

She took a deep breath and picked up her pencil. If ever she needed reassurance, a reminder that she wasn't growing weaker, that phone call had certainly given it to her. Love, hope, agony, all awoke within her at the very thought of seeing her son again. He was what was important, was where her emotions lay. She neeedn't worry that she was going to get all soft and clinging with Ryan and lose sight of her real goals. Maybe she could continue the friendship without a worry.

"Have you ever had Vietnamese food?" Ryan asked that evening.

Val fought to drag her consciousness back from the far corner of her mind where it had been hiding. "No. No, I haven't," she said, and reached out for another piece of pizza. At least it would give her something to hold onto.

"A few of us had it for lunch today," Ryan went on. "It was real good. We'll have to try it sometime."

"All right."

Her words sounded so stiff. Poor Ryan, she thought. He had been carrying the bulk of the conversation all night, but somehow she couldn't think of a thing to say. She couldn't tell him what was in her heart, the agony of missing her son, and she didn't know how to bring up last night either.

She searched for something else to say. "Have you talked to your kids tonight?" she asked.

Ryan shook his head. "It's not working out to call them each evening. I was told I was hampering their social activities by expecting them to hang around the house for my call."

She couldn't help but smile.

"I'm allowed to call on Wednesday evenings and if they have a problem some other time, they'll call me. So far, no emergency's come up though. Mrs. Ricco is a real gem."

"That's good."

"Thanks to you." Ryan raised his wine glass to her. "My family affairs are under control and everybody's happy."

They fell into a pit of silence again. Her son had been on her mind all day. Was she setting herself up for a fall by hoping for so much this time? At times she was tempted to confide in Ryan, to share her hopes and fears with him, but the habit of silence was hard to break.

"The pizza's all gone."

His words brought her back out, peering cautiously over the edge into the present reality. The box stood empty, stray bits of cheese and crust sticking to it. It indeed was gone and two little cats were sniffing around the edges.

"If you're still hungry we can call for some more, I suppose," she said.

His eyes were looking at her, laying on a soft mantle of concern around her shoulders, but he shook his head. "I've had more than enough," he replied and reached for the wine bottle. "There's still some of this left. Want your glass topped off?"

Val frowned into her glass, still half full. "I don't think so."

"Are you going to make me drink it all?" Ryan asked. "What kind of a friend are you? I'm the one who has to drive home."

She smiled with reluctance and pushed her glass forward. Of course, Ryan wouldn't have to drive home, a little voice reminded her, but she said nothing. He filled her glass, then drained the last few drops into his own. He really deserved better treatment than she'd been giving him.

"Thank you," she murmured.

He nodded and sipped his wine. She took a drink from her glass, then examined the fingers gripping her glass. "We have a good friendship," she said.

"We have?" One eyebrow was raised, giving emphasis to his question. "I'm glad to hear you put it in the present tense. After this morning, I wasn't sure what your thoughts on the matter were."

"So much had happened," Val said. "I was afraid."

Ryan pushed his glass aside and took one of her hands in both of his. "We had a weekend together. What happened was a natural physical phenomenon. There was nothing to be afraid of. If adding a physical relationship to our friendship works out, that's fine with me. If it doesn't, I'm still your friend."

Val cupped his hands in hers, holding them tightly. "I realize that now. I did a lot of thinking today. It wasn't the making love that made me afraid, but my reaction to it. I've been in love before and burned. I'm not going to let it happen again."

"That's the way I feel, too," Ryan said.

She nodded, gathering courage and speed from the gentle understanding in his eyes. "I wasn't sure I was strong enough to keep my heart intact," she admitted. "And I thought that maybe the safest way to stay unscathed was to stay away from you."

Ryan waited. His eyes remained gentle, though a flicker of sadness could be seen in their depths. She smiled at him and made the decision. He was her friend and what were friends for, if not for confiding?

She took a deep breath. "But then I realized that the trick to being your friend, with all that it now entails, and not falling into the love trap, was to focus on where my heart lies."

That flicker of sadness, of concern deepened. "You're in love with someone else?"

She shook her head. "Not like you mean," she said quickly and then looked into the depths of his eyes. "You see, I have a son."

He blinked once, but nothing else changed. The eyes remained sad, but his expression was gentle and understanding. "He lives with his father?"

She closed her eyes for a moment and let her hands cling to his. "I don't know where he lives. I haven't seen him since he was born."

Some questions crept into his eyes, but they stayed gentle.

"I was a freshman in college." She swallowed the lump that wanted to grow. "I wasn't very popular. Didn't have many friends. So, when this guy—he was captain of the football team—came on to me, I just—" Val shrugged "—I was overwhelmed."

He nodded.

"We moved into a small apartment off campus. I was in heaven." She couldn't keep the disgust from her voice.

"You were just a kid."

Val shook her head. She didn't need him to make excuses for her; she'd accepted the truth by this point. "I was stupid." She took a deep breath and sat up straighter. "I didn't use any kind of birth control."

"So the two of you had a baby."

"*I* had a baby. He was long gone before the event, shacking up with some other little mouse. I was immature and had no resources of any kind—family, money, internal strength—nothing.''

"You put him up for adoption."

Val nodded. The lump in her throat wanted to overpower her and spill tears from her eyes, but she wouldn't let it. Ryan allowed her to pull strength from him. "You did what was best for him and for you."

She nodded again. "I guess."

"So you were wrong just now."

Val looked at him blankly.

"You must have had enormous internal strength to give him up."

"I had no choice."

"There's always choices. You could have had an abortion."

But Val just pulled away from him, claiming her hands and leaning back in her chair. "No, I couldn't have done that. I loved him, even unborn and unwanted, at least by his father."

"And you love him still? The boy, I mean. I presume your feelings for the football captain are long since dead."

Val nodded. "Even the anger has left. But yes, my son will always have my heart." Talking about him seemed to release a chain keeping her heart a prisoner. Tears welled up in her eyes, but the aching pain that thinking of the boy always brought was milder, more distant than usual.

Ryan released her hands to come sit next to her on the sofa, his arms a safe haven from the pain of the world, and she gladly went into them. "If your son has your heart, maybe it's all the more reason you need a good friend," he said softly. "One who understands and won't ask more from you than you can give."

"I am lucky to have found you," she whispered even as his lips came down to hers.

"We're both lucky," Ryan murmured.

Chapter Ten

Val pulled her yellow plastic bracelets off of her wrist and threw them down onto the dresser. Damn! She should have just stayed at the office tonight; she still had a mountain of work to catch up on. Yesterday had not been the most productive beginning to a week and today had been only marginally better. There was no reason on earth for her and Ryan to go out tonight.

Sighing, Val took off her earrings. It wasn't really a date, so there was no reason for her to dress up. Even if it were a date, she shouldn't really dress up. They were just going to the park to hear a summer concert series given by the Fort Wayne Civic Orchestra. It was an informal event where people dressed however they felt comfortable.

They were only two friends spending a pleasant evening together, listening to some music. It didn't matter whether Ryan was a male or female friend. Then a fire began to smolder in the pit of her stomach as the yellow bracelets winked in mockery at her. Sure, it didn't matter, a little voice agreed. His broad shoulders didn't affect her at all and nothing about his embrace made her heart beat one iota faster. She angrily pushed the jewelry aside and went outside to wait for Ryan.

The evening was warm, but pleasantly so. There was a lazy summer feel to the air, a sultriness that soon had her muddled emotions calm. She sat on the low wall by the parking lot, watching for Ryan's car. The topsy-turvy state of her thoughts wasn't like her. She was level-headed and calm, not given to flights of fancy and indecision. It couldn't be Ryan who was doing this to her. It had to be Chambliss's call.

That thought calmed her enough so that when Ryan's car pulled into the lot, she stood waving him over. He stopped the car in front of her and Val stepped in quickly, not giving him a chance to come out and open the door for her. She was better now, strong enough to realize that two friends, who just happened to be going out together, didn't need to fool with such silly formalities as the man opening the door for the woman.

"We have a lot of time," Ryan said. "You didn't have to wait outside for me."

They didn't have a lot of time. They had too much time. Too much time to fill with idle conversation while they sat around her home.

"It's such a pleasant evening," Val said brightly. "And I was tired of being cooped up all day, so I decided to wait outside."

Ryan nodded. "It is nice out. Good for a concert." He smiled at her. "Or any number of things."

Val felt her stomach tighten up and she looked at Ryan. He didn't turn toward her though, but must have felt the heat of her gaze, for he quickly added, "Walking down by the river, boating, dinner at an outdoor café. Stuff like that."

She let her eyes swing to the front so she could look out the car window. That was why they shouldn't have become lovers. It certainly had its advantages, but it complicated their friendship. She misinterpreted everything he said.

"A nickel for your thoughts."

Val raised an eyebrow in his direction.

"Hey," he protested. "That's a five hundred percent increase from the usual offer."

"I'm not sure that I have any thoughts," Val said, with a sigh. "All I have is bits and pieces swirling around. It's very confusing at the moment." They rode the rest of the way in silence, but it was a comfortable one.

Once they had parked, Ryan walked around to the trunk and took out a blanket, two back supporters and a small cooler, and put them all on the ground. By that time, Val had convinced herself she was ready for an evening of enjoyment, with nothing to worry about or fuss over.

"Goodness," she said with a laugh. "You certainly come well prepared."

"Ex-boy scout," he muttered as he checked the trunk for any stray items. "Always prepared, etc., etc."

"Anything else you have in there?" she asked.

"Oh, just a few items. A life raft, flashlight, hip boots."

She caught a glimpse of a rather empty trunk just before he slammed it shut and made a face at him. "You're joking."

"You'll never know," he replied. "Make yourself useful and grab something."

"Yes, sir." She picked up the blanket, following Ryan into the park. The air smelled sweetly of trees and freshly mowed lawn. The laughter and chatter of people around them sounded like the song of the wind in the trees.

Ryan turned and waited for her to catch up. "I have a favorite spot," he told her. "Close enough to hear, but far enough not to be bugged by a lot of people."

"Sounds good." But a shadow crossed her heart. Was it his favorite spot or, as would be more likely, had it been his and Maggie's favorite spot? That thought was unworthy of her, Val scolded herself, and pushed it out of her mind. Everyone came into this world with baggage and they picked up more as they went along. Besides, a friend was someone who accepted you and your baggage. Jealousy arose only when hearts were involved.

Ryan spread the blanket, then pulled lemonade out of the cooler. "Sorry about the lack of wine," he said. "But they don't allow alcoholic beverages in the park."

"Lemonade will be just fine."

There were also some cherry tarts, their sweetness serving as a successful counterpoint to the tartness of the lemon. Val leaned back against the back supporters, closed her eyes and let the pleasant mood of the music wash over her. Ryan took her hand in his. She stiffened momentarily as memories of the other night washed over her, but then she relaxed.

Ryan was right. This was an ideal spot to listen to the music. And it wasn't just the fact that it was quiet, with fewer people. It was far enough away from the band so that the music wasn't overpowering.

The soft breeze guided the notes and danced with them. Sometimes fast, sometimes slow. It all depended on the tempo of the music. They all combined to form a circle around the couple, keeping the cares of the everyday world away. Business concerns were easily kept at bay, and as for her son, Val was sure that issue was going to be resolved. She didn't know how, but she was sure that soon it would no longer be a worry.

Ryan was also within that circle and he should have been an intruder, but he wasn't. Rather someone to share the quiet moments with, not someone to add to the worries.

Soon after the music began dusk arrived. Then came the stars. Finally, after a couple of hours of Eden, the world reappeared. The music ended and the regular world of people talking, lawn chairs scraping on the parking lot surface, and the smell of auto exhaust fumes enveloped them. They picked up their things, balancing them so that they could still walk hand in hand back to Ryan's car. Neither spoke. The silence was too perfect and precious somehow; Val couldn't bear to break it with the mundane woes of life. Before she knew it, Ryan pulled up in front of her door.

"Want to come up?" she asked.

He shook his head. "It's late and I'm flying to Washington D.C., tomorrow. I've got to get home and pack."

"You're leaving?" Her heart had skipped a beat, her stomach sank and storm clouds covered her smile. "How long are you going to be gone?"

"Enough for you to miss me, I hope," he teased and, leaning forward, kissed her lightly on the lips.

He got out of the car then and hurried around to open her door. Val felt too depressed suddenly to play at her games of independence, climbing out slowly. "Come on," she said. "How long are you really going to be gone?"

"Just one day," he said. "I leave early tomorrow and come back late in the evening. Then we can go up to the lake again Friday, if you're game."

"Oh, I don't know. I probably ought to stay here and get some work done," she said evasively.

"You can't. It's Casey's birthday this Saturday. She'll be crushed if you don't come."

"But that's a family thing. You don't want an outsider butting in."

He kissed her again, a deep and dark hinting of magic. "You're a friend and she would like you there. See you on Friday?"

She nodded slowly. "Yes, all right. Have a good trip."

Then he was gone and she leaned against the door, watching his car leave the parking lot, letting her eyes follow the twin red lights until they disappeared up the road. Damn. She was going to miss him.

"I'm just going to be out for an hour or two, guys," Val told her cats the next evening.

Yang lifted his head up to glare at her; Yin didn't even bother. "Aw, please don't cry," Val said, mockingly. "You'll make me sad."

She gave them a glare of her own as Yang dropped his head back down. The two fuzz balls were curled up around each other, taking their early evening nap. It looked as if they were going to handle her absence very well.

"Yeah, I know," Val muttered. "Shut the door on my way out." Yang flickered an ear at her.

Val was still shaking her head as she got into her car. Cats! They sure knew how to make a person feel needed. But wasn't that what she wanted? a little voice asked. Needing no one and no one needing her?

Darn right it was, Val answered back, giving herself a mental pat on the back as she pulled out of the lot. Ryan had left this morning on his business trip, but she was not sitting around moping and missing him. Nope, she had realized that she was becoming far too dependent on him for companionship and that wasn't a good thing. Sure, it was nice to have a special friend, but if that special friend became your *only* friend, then you had a problem.

Val was an independent woman, fully able to care for herself, but with Ryan around she'd become a little lazy. It was a good thing that he was on a trip. He should take more of them. Now that he had a dependable house-keeper, he probably would. She pulled onto the main street.

She and Ryan really had gotten into too many things together. It wasn't that he was the only person in her life; he'd just become a habit. Well, habits were made and habits were broken. It was now time for her to break the Ryan Crawford habit. Not entirely, but she had to let other things into her life. After all, she'd found him a housekeeper so he could spend more time on his business. Now she needed to spend more time on hers, some of which was maintaining contacts.

A purplish neon cow winked at her in the distance. Thursday night was the usual get-together evening for her friends from the tennis club. She hadn't seen them in a while and it would be fun to renew acquaintances.

The Purple Ox wasn't too crowded and Val found her friends at a large round table in the back. There were some new faces since she'd been here the last time, but that was no problem. That was one of the things she liked about this group, its ever-changing array of faces.

She cleared her throat and walked the last few steps. "Hi, guys."

The group of men and women around the large round table paused momentarily in their multiple conversations to stare at her. "Val?"

"Hi, Val."

The chorus of greetings built up until all had welcomed her. She pulled a chair from another table and squeezed into their group.

"I'll have a glass of Rhine," she told the passing waitress. "Anybody else want anything?"

They shook their heads, most of them returning to their previous conversations as Val endured an uncomfortable few moments of eavesdropping as she waited for her drink. There was a new tennis pro at the club. The pro shop had a new line of sportswear that was the absolute latest. The club was going to be closed for a week in November for the courts to be resurfaced.

Her wine came and she took a large sip before forcing herself to speak when there was a pause in the conversation next to her. "So," she said, with gusto, "how have things been going for all of you?"

There were shrugs all around.

"All right."

"Not bad."

"Same old stuff."

The store of information was quickly exhausted and the group nearest her began a discussion of the Wimbledon tournament. Val was beginning to feel like a stranger or, worse yet, like the kid no one in school liked. The one who was allowed to sit at the table only because the teacher had insisted on it.

"Where have you been keeping yourself?" the woman on the other side of Val asked.

"Work mostly," Val replied.

"Every night?"

Val nodded. "Not to mention the weekends."

"You working on your second million?" someone else asked.

Val felt as if she were being backed into a corner. "I had some tough problems," she stammered.

"Oh," they chorused.

She nodded again and they fell back into silence. Her glass was almost empty. This wasn't quite going as she'd planned, but that was no problem. It was too easy to make conversation with Ryan. She needed more practice with others.

"Were you at the summer concert Tuesday night?" her neighbor asked suddenly.

"Summer concert?" Val was almost tempted to say no, but then why should she lie? "Yes, I was."

"I thought it was you."

She could see the question blazing out of the woman's eyes. And who were you with? "I went with a client," Val told her.

The woman said nothing.

"He was a very difficult case," Val went on to explain. "A widower with three children. It took me weeks to find the right housekeeper for him."

"You certainly take care of your clients."

"Service," Val said, with a laugh, an annoyingly squeaky laugh. "That's really all I have to offer."

The woman nodded solemnly. Val's glass was now empty and her throat felt dry. What was she doing here?

There was no one here she could talk to, no one who cared whether she came or not.

"Care for another drink, Val?" A couple of them ordered beers and the waitress stopped to stare at Val. "No. No, thank you," she said, standing up. "I have some shopping to do. I just stopped by to say hi to everybody."

"Don't be a stranger, Val."

"Oh, I won't," she assured them. "Things are under control now so I'll be back playing tennis again."

"Good."

Val breathed a huge sigh of relief once she was back in her car. That had been a disaster. Not that they weren't nice people, but she just didn't have anything to say to them. They weren't close at all. If they had been, it would have hurt for her to be separated from them. Like it did now to be apart from Ryan.

She shook her head. She had to stop fighting all this. It was normal to miss a friend, normal to think of them when they weren't around and to be preoccupied with them when they were. Nothing was free. To have a friend, you had to be a friend, to open yourself up. But when you opened yourself up, your defenses were down and then it was easier to get hurt.

"Hell," she swore as she turned on the ignition. She was going to buy herself some new shoes.

But an hour later she was still wandering the mall looking in windows. None of them had anything she wanted. She wasn't really sure what she wanted, but she was sure no one had it. She might as well go home. Maybe Yin and Yang would let her watch television.

As she was passing through a large department store on her way to the parking lot, a large floppy-looking stuffed dog caught her eye. Casey's birthday was this

Saturday. There were shelves of stuffed animals in the girl's room, but none that looked like this dog.

Val hesitated. Would Ryan be angry if she bought his daughter a present before clearing it with him? Would he think she was trying to make something more of their simple, straightforward little friendship? She turned to walk away.

She took one step. The kids were her friends, too. And Casey had shared her room with Val. Val marched into the toy department and bought the dog. She was still smiling with pleasure from her purchase when she got home.

"This is for Casey," she told the two cats as she put the bag on the table. They jumped up and sniffed at it.

"It's a dog." Val thought that they'd stiffened for a moment. "I mean it's a stuffed dog." She took it out of the bag for them to inspect.

"Casey is a nice kid," she told the cats as they circled the dog carefully. "You guys would probably like her." Yang gave her a highly skeptical look. "I mean it. I'll bring her around sometime."

Val kicked off her shoes and checked her answering machine. The blinking light indicated one message. Val hoped it wasn't someone with a problem. She wasn't up to dashing out anyplace tonight. Reluctantly she played back the message.

"Hi."

Ryan's soft voice seized her. Damn. Why hadn't she stayed home?

"Sorry I missed you," he said. "I have a meeting that's going to go late into the evening, so I had to move my flight back. I won't be getting in until midnight, so it'll be too late to call you once I get home. I'll call you tomorrow at work. Bye. Miss you."

The machine hummed derisively at her. She reset it and walked slowly into the living room, dropping down onto the sofa. Damn, double damn. She should have stayed home. She and the Purple Ox group didn't have that much in common anymore. Not that they were ever more than casual friends. Not like she and Ryan. They were special friends.

She sighed and stared up at the cathedral ceiling. That had its good points and ... its less than good points.

"Have a pleasant evening, sir."

Ryan tried but couldn't quite match the wattage of the flight attendant's smile. In fact, he was sure that he hadn't even come close. Ah, the hell with it.

It had been a very productive day, but he sure couldn't take too many of them. Not at his age. Only a college kid could stand the nonstop activity and then look forward to about four hours of sleep.

His feet carried him out into the main terminal area without any thought on his part. He shuffled along, head down. He hoped it wouldn't be too hard to find a cab. He was barely in shape to walk, and if he couldn't find one quickly, maybe he'd just go to the airport hotel and bed down. He could take a cab to the office in the morning.

"Hi."

Ryan grunted and continued walking.

"Ryan?"

He stopped, turned and tried to focus his bleary eyes. "Val." It took a mighty effort but he finally pushed the name out past his lips. "What are you doing here?"

She shrugged. "I wasn't doing anything else so I thought I might as well come get you."

He rubbed his eyes. "I was going to take a cab."

She frowned at him. "I see," she said. "So do you want to change your plans and ride with me or should I go home and let you contribute to cab drivers' employment?"

He smiled. "I'll take the ride."

She fell into step beside him. "Let me help you with your bags," she said.

"No," he said rather loudly. "They're heavy. I can handle them."

"Stop being so macho." She laughed. "Here, I'll take this little one." She took the small bag that kept slipping off his shoulder. "Were you planning on staying away a couple of months?"

Ryan shook his head. "I've got only a few of my own things. Most of the rest is ad mock-ups and that kind of stuff."

They walked in silence out to the parking lot. "How did you know I needed a ride?" he asked as he waited for her to unlock her van. "I might have driven here."

"Lucky you didn't. You can barely keep your eyes open now," she said with a snicker.

"You didn't answer my question," he protested.

"I drove by your house and looked in the garage."

"Boy," he grumbled. "Give you an inch and you move right in and take over, don't you?"

"Service is our business," she said, giving him a wide smile.

Ryan slouched down in the seat, certain he was pleased by her thoughtfulness, but not certain he ought to be. He probably ought to put his foot down with Val. He shouldn't let her take over everything in his life.

Maybe he'd do it tomorrow, he told himself as he closed his eyes against the brightness of the oncoming cars. Friendship was one thing, but—

Damn it! Why did she keep poking him? "What?" he snapped.

"Time to get out, Sleeping Beauty." Her voice had a gratingly cheerful lilt to it. "You're home."

Blinking, he stared about. They were sitting in his driveway, right behind his car, up by the garage. "Sorry," he mumbled. "I was thinking about that Big Brothers/Big Sisters campaign."

"Sure."

"I was."

"Don't be so testy," she said. "I'm not arguing."

"Good," he mumbled. Ryan stared around the interior of the van. His damn eyes wanted to fuzz up again. "Where are my bags?"

"I have them" she said from where she stood in the driveway. "Now, would you please open the door?"

By the time he got out of the car, she was halfway up the front steps, a large bag in each hand and the small bag hanging from her shoulders. Slamming his door, Ryan made it up the steps without stumbling and unlocked his front door.

"Ladies first," he said, bowing slightly.

"Thank you." She dropped the bags in the hall.

"Would you like a glass of wine?" he asked.

"Did you have dinner?"

Ryan frowned. He thought he was asking the questions. "No. We sent out for something at the meeting, but I never got around to eating it. Then they had some kind of snack on the plane I couldn't identify, and my father always told me if you can't name it, don't eat it."

"I have some soup and fresh bread for you. It'll help you sleep if you've got something in your stomach," she said. "Come in the kitchen and eat it."

"Did my mother pass away while I was gone?" he asked.

She stopped at the kitchen door. "No. Why do you ask?"

"I don't know. It looks like you're taking over the job."

Ryan wasn't sure, but he thought Val was frowning. Her soup was wonderful though, hot and delicious. Enough to take the edge off the hunger he'd been surprised to find.

"Thank you, ma'am."

"Service is our game," she replied brightly.

Her yellow pedal pushers and yellow sleeveless blouse accented her curves quite nicely. She'd kicked off her sandals, perching on the high kitchen stool like a bright little canary. Now that he was home and had eaten, he wasn't so tired anymore. He took her hand in his.

"Why don't we go in the den and watch television or just talk?"

That beautiful smile of hers lit up her face and his heart. "I think bed would be a better idea."

Desire and adrenaline surged through his body. Not only had the tiredness left his body, but Ryan knew that he couldn't sleep anyway. He put on a smile to match the one Val wore.

"I mean for you alone," she said. "So you can get all the sleep you need."

He couldn't believe he had heard her right. "You're leaving?"

"Yep." She stepped into her sandals.

"I thought we were friends." He didn't like the plaintive tone that his voice carried, but now that the words were out it was too late to do anything about it.

"We are," she said softly as she kissed him on the cheek. She walked to the door, turned to give him a smile and a wave, and then she was gone. Tiredness came back to reclaim all his cells, but that didn't mean that sleep would come.

Chapter Eleven

When they stopped for the traffic light Ryan quickly glanced over his shoulder. "The kids are going to be peeved with me."

"Why?"

"They're going to insist I brought the rain with me," he replied, indicating the menacing darkness looming in the distance behind them.

"That's not your fault." The words sounded so lame and stupid. Even the kids would know that the rain wasn't Ryan's fault, though there wasn't a kid in the world who could resist the chance to hassle their father a bit. Val turned to stare out the window. Since when had she become such an expert on child psychology? One childbearing did not a parent make.

She still wasn't sure she should be going to the cottage this weekend, but then how could she refuse a plea from Casey, passed along through Ryan, to come help celebrate her birthday? Sighing, Val looked out her window. Going up for Casey's birthday was hardly as big a deal as going to the airport in the middle of the night to pick up Ryan. If she was worried that she was giving the wrong impression, maybe she ought to start looking at all her actions.

Stray raindrops were starting to fall, large drops that left big blotches on the glass. Maybe if the rain got there before them, the kids wouldn't accuse Ryan of bringing it along and they'd all stay friends.

Friends. Val had had many friends over the years, but she'd never found a friendship as complicated as this one.

"It's getting dark," Ryan said as he switched on the headlights.

It was, in more ways than one.

By the time she and Ryan had pulled into the cottage yard, the rain was pouring down in what they called a gully washer back in Texas. Lately Texas had been on her mind a great deal. Chambliss hadn't called yet, so he must still be following his lead. He'd said he wouldn't call until he had run the trail down to its very end, but that didn't mean that she could stop thinking about him.

She sighed and tried to put it out of her mind for the moment at least as the kids crowded around the car. They had either just come from swimming or had been playing in the rain; they were wearing their swimsuits and their hair was hanging down in wet mops. Val felt a lump rise in her throat at the smiles on their faces. Would her son ever smile like that at her?

"You guys are getting all wet," Ryan scolded.

"Dad," Casey said, patience oozing to mix with the water flowing down her body. "It's just like going swimming."

The boys made swimming motions with their arms and Val couldn't help but laugh. She was glad she'd come. The weekend here would take the edge off waiting.

Casey snatched Val's bag, leaving the twins to settle for Ryan's, then follow her, not dropping their load more than once or twice. Val kicked off her sandals, letting her bare feet enjoy the cool puddles that the quick downpour had created. She felt the strain of the last few days wash away as a giggling sense of high spirits took over her soul.

"Come on, Val," Ryan urged. "You're going to get soaked just like the kids."

"Oh, Dad," Casey protested. "Don't be an old fuddy-duddy."

A horrified look crossed Ryan's eyes, but he slowed his pace to walk with Val toward the house. "I'm getting a little tired of this old fuddy-duddy nonsense," he muttered.

"I didn't say anything," Val pointed out with a sweet smile. "It's your daughter who seems to have that image of you."

"Yes, but you could help. You know, point out how wise I am or how handsome, from time to time."

"I guess I could do that," she agreed with apparent serious consideration, but then a grin crept out. "You are pretty good-looking for an old fuddy-duddy."

"Val!"

But Val had taken flight, rushing into the house just ahead of the kids, forcing Ryan to come in behind them. He was wet and pretending a rage that had them all laughing.

"I've had it with fuddy-duddy remarks," he bellowed once inside. "Now all of you, get out of your wet clothes, and when you come back, start remembering how young I am.''

There were snickers to be heard, but the kids all obediently trooped down to their rooms. Val started to follow, but Ryan grabbed her hand to keep her there.

''Fuddy-duddy indeed,'' he murmured and pulled her into his arms.

His lips were rough and demanding but woke a sleeping flame in her soul. Stronger, hotter, more encompassing than ever before, the fires of desire raged through her, singeing her heart and consuming her soul. His mouth moved over hers in sweet possession but breathless delight was her only response. The magic of his embrace was her whole world.

''There now,'' he said as he pulled slowly away. ''Was that the kiss of an old fuddy-duddy?''

''No, sir,'' she said softly. Reluctant to let his lips leave, she kissed him again gently, then again. ''Not even a young fuddy-duddy.''

''Respect, woman,'' he said with a laugh. ''That's all I want, a little respect.''

''That's what I thought you were getting,'' she said. ''A little respect. Very little.''

He sighed and let her escape his arms completely. ''Go change out of your wet clothes before you catch a cold.''

Val kissed him once more, a teasing, friendly kiss, then obeyed. Casey was already changed when she got into the room and the girl was drying her hair.

''You got your hair cut and permed,'' Val said as she pulled dry clothes from her bag.

Casey turned to face her. ''Yeah,'' the girl said with a grin. ''It's just like yours.''

Val stopped in surprise, a sudden glow warming her heart. ''It looks very nice.''

"Thank you," Casey said and went back to drying it.

Val watched Casey for a long moment before she finally shook herself into motion. This friendship, certainly brought some surprises along with it. She finished dressing quietly and then dried her own hair.

Mrs. Ricco made a delicious dinner of whitefish sauteed in wine sauce, baked potatoes and broccoli, accompanied by grumbles from the children. The housekeeper admonished Casey and the twins saying that they couldn't have hot dogs or spaghetti all the time. Val concentrated on her food, trying to work her way through the maze of thoughts. Even the bickering was becoming familiar and comfortable now. But was all this good or bad?

"The children will help me clean up the dishes before I'm on my way," Mrs. Ricco announced after dinner. "The two of you can go sit on the porch and relax."

"Oh, that wouldn't be fair," Val protested. "I can help."

"That's right," Richard said. "It ain't fair."

"Yeah," Robert chimed in.

"Your father and Miss Dennison work hard all week," the housekeeper said sternly. "The rest of us laze around in the sun."

"That's okay," Val said. "I don't—"

"Out." Mrs. Ricco put on a forbidding expression and pointed toward the porch.

"Come on," Ryan said, taking Val's hand. "Let's get out of here before you cause any more trouble."

"What kind of trouble am I causing?" His hand was awfully comfortable to hold, like a lifeline that would keep her sane this weekend. More than that actually, happy and smiling.

"Aggravating my housekeeper," Ryan said. "That's very serious. I'd consider it a felony if you caused her to leave."

"She wouldn't leave."

But Val's mind was not really on her words. Ryan was leading her to a rustic love seat made out of rough-cut planking and cushions. "Just what are you planning?"

He sat and pulled her down next to him. "Mrs. Ricco told us to relax and I follow orders well."

"That's good to know," Val said, pulling at the arm around her waist. "I order you to take your arm off and go sit on your—"

"Did I mention that I obey only certain people?"

Val relaxed her pulling and concentrated all her energy in a frown. "And just which certain people, or need I ask?"

"Well, Mrs. Ricco is one."

His eyes danced with mischief like those of his two little boys, and as with her reaction to the boys, Val vacillated between wanting to swat him and hug him. She'd just about decided on the hug, when a little voice spoke from behind her.

"How come you guys are always hanging on each other?"

The boys walked onto the porch, a grinning Casey following. Val didn't know which twin had asked the question.

"We're not hanging on each other," Ryan said. "We're friends and friends like to sit close to each other."

"If you sat any closer," Robert said, "you guys would be all mushed into one."

Ryan relaxed his grasp and Val slowly slid over to her end of the love seat. The kids grinned even more as if not fooled by the maneuver.

"Can we go outside, Dad?" Richard asked.

"No," he replied. "It's still raining."

"We won't melt," Robert assured him.

Val saw flashes out over the lake. "There's lightning," she said. "It wouldn't be a good idea to run around outside."

Both boys looked glumly outside as another flash and the accompanying thunder gave emphasis to her words. Val understood their confusion. It was hard to accept that something fun could also be something dangerous, just like sitting here on the love seat with Ryan. Already her heart was whispering suggestions to her hands, suggestions her hands were just itching to follow.

"Let's play Monopoly," Casey suggested.

"That's a good idea," Val said, jumping to her feet. Anything to stay occupied.

Ryan slowly dragged his body up. "I hate games," he muttered.

She didn't. Not anymore. There were some games she was learning to enjoy very much.

Val was out in a garden, dancing with Ryan to a slow, sweet melody that she couldn't quite hear, but could feel all the way down in her soul. In his arms, she swayed to the beat, moving to a gentle rhythm that urged them closer and closer. Until Casey came outside also, shining a glaring flashlight as she called Val's name.

"Val, wake up."

The garden faded and so did the light into the early morning sun. Val opened her eyes slowly. "Casey?" It was just starting to get light outside. "What's wrong?"

"Nothing," the girl replied. "I just thought you might want to go to the bathroom and get dressed."

Val frowned at the girl and stared at the digital clock on the windowsill. "It's not even six o'clock." What in the world was wrong with Casey?

"I know," Casey said, looking slightly apologetic. "But Dad's going to bring me breakfast in bed in a few minutes and I didn't know if you'd want to be in just your nightshirt when he comes in."

Why not? Ryan had seen her in less. The thought brought a blush to Val's cheeks, but Casey appeared not to notice.

"It's my birthday," Casey went on to explain, patience filling her voice. "And in our family the birthday person always gets breakfast in bed."

"Oh." Val rubbed her eyes and let her feet down to the floor. "That's nice."

Casey frowned though. "I probably should have told them I'd have my breakfast in the kitchen this year," she said. "It's not fair to make you get up this early."

"Oh, no." Val jumped up from the bed. She was not about to spoil Casey's birthday treat. "I always get up this early. I was just a little surprised, that's all."

"Are you sure?"

"No problem," Val said, pasting a smile on her lips and heading for the door. "I'll just dash into the bathroom and then throw something on. It'll be fine."

Val dashed down the hallway. Adult murmurs and youthful giggles floated out from the kitchen, following her down to the bathroom. Crawford birthday breakfasts must be a family affair.

Now that she was awake, Val knew that she wouldn't have ruined Casey's traditional celebration for anything in the world. Family traditions were important.

They'd give Casey pleasant memories for the rest of her life. Val's parents had never been into anything like that and she'd learned not to expect anything from her various foster parents. Most of them hadn't even known when her birthday was, though one family, the Tylers, had taken her out to dinner the birthday she was with them. That had been nice. Val splashed cold water on her face, dedicating her day to the goddess of cheerfulness. She hurried back into the bedroom and threw on a shirt and shorts.

"It sounds like they're almost ready," Casey whispered. "I should warn you that my brothers tend to get rowdy on birthdays and it doesn't matter whose it is."

Val barely had time to finger comb her curls before there was a loud knock on the door. "Ready or not, here we come." It was Ryan's voice, but the twins burst in first.

Casey was right. The boys were well on their way to bouncing off the walls. Ryan set the tray with blueberry pancakes in front of Casey, then all sang "Happy Birthday." The twins charged in and out of the room while Val and Ryan sat down to chat.

After breakfast Casey went on to open her presents. The boys had bought her earrings, an individually wrapped single earring from each. Ryan gave her a new clock radio in a pink so hot it looked like it would glow in the dark. Casey threw her arms around him in delight, then opened Val's present.

"Oh," the girl exclaimed over the stuffed dog. "He's so cute. I just love him." She reached over to hug Val with what looked to be the same fervor with which she'd hugged her father.

Val shrugged, embarrassment over Casey's emotions robbing her of sense. "I just saw him when I was shopping."

Casey hugged the floppy dog tightly to herself. "I'm going to name him Valentino."

"I was looking for shoes," Val explained further, trying to clear a lump from her throat.

There was a moment of quiet as Casey basked in the love of her family. Val watched through a blur and the pain returned to her throat, pain from the lack of memories from her own childhood and the lack of ones she'd given her son.

"Well, kid," Ryan said, breaking the silence. "What's on the agenda for today?"

"Cedar Point," Casey replied to the boys' enthusiastic cheering.

Val's stomach was concerned. She'd heard of the amusement park, but had never been there. Hurtling upside down on a narrow roller coaster track wasn't her idea of fun—or her stomach's.

"Maybe I should stay here and keep an eye on the house," she offered an hour later as they drove away from the house.

"What for?" Ryan asked. "It likely to walk away if we aren't here?"

"I guess not."

He gave her a sharp look. "Don't you like amusement parks?"

"I don't go to them that much." Her stomach fluttered. Ryan smiled. Val knew he was trying to be reassuring, but she slouched back in her seat. Maybe they would have four flat tires. Maybe they would get lost.

By the time they'd pulled in the entrance to the amusement park Val was eager to get out. They'd started with a hundred bottles of beer on the wall, but she was sure that at least three hundred thousand had fallen before they turned in the Cedar Point entrance.

"All right, what's the plan?" Ryan asked as they gathered just inside the entrance.

"I want to go on that," Robert said, pointing to the Demon Drop, a huge tower from which a small car of riders plunged straight down.

"That looks like a good way to die," Val said, her face paling at the very thought of going on it.

"Val, nobody gets hurt on these things," Casey assured her. "The rides are all tested for safety."

"I wasn't talking about accidents on the rides," Val pointed out. "I was talking about heart failure."

"Heart failure?" Ryan mocked though he put his arm around Val's shoulder protectively. "And you called *me* an old fuddy-duddy."

So of course the rest of the day was spent putting Val to the test. She liked the bumper cars and the train ride, but around every corner there seemed to be another roller coaster.

"Come on, Val," one of them would say. "This one is tame."

They'd beg and plead and cajole until she agreed to try it, somehow always with Ryan. She'd get strapped into place, her hand clutching Ryan's for dear life. Then death would rush up to laugh in her face before the ride eased to a stop.

"Wasn't that fun?" they'd all ask as Ryan peeled her off the seat and practically carried her down the stairs to the sidewalk.

"Great," she'd insist. "See? I'm no fuddy-duddy either."

"Why are you shaking?" Robert would ask.

"And hugging Daddy so tight?" Richard would follow with.

"I like him," Val would say, and they'd all grin and go on to another ride.

She liked the water rides. Getting splashed on a warm summer's day was always a treat. And the shows were fun. But best of all was just the way they all laughed together. She didn't even mind the roller coasters; there was no malice involved, just good-natured teasing that showed how well the kids accepted her. The day passed into evening all too quickly.

"Hey, look what's up there," Richard called out suddenly as they neared the exit. It was the awful-looking Demon Drop.

"Val's had enough," Ryan said, coming to her rescue before they even fell into the routine.

"Aw, Dad, it doesn't look so scary," Robert argued.

"You must need your eyesight checked," Val said. "It looks terrible. This is one fuddy-duddy who's sitting out."

"And this another," Ryan said.

"You guys are no fun," Robert muttered, but Casey took the boys by the hand.

"Come on, guys, we can go on it without parental supervision." She glanced for a moment at Ryan and Val, her eyes glittering with mirth. "And I bet it'll cause a lifelong trauma that only a double dip ice-cream cone will heal."

Ryan pulled Val over to a nearby bench.

"Your kids are fun," she told him as they sank onto the bench with stereophonic sighs. "I can't remember when I've had such fun."

"You've been an awfully good sport. You didn't have to let them bully you into all those roller coaster rides."

Val yawned and let her head rest on his conveniently close shoulder. "I'll have you know I wasn't bullied into anything. I can say *no* quite well when I want to."

"You didn't seem too thrilled about some of those rides."

"It was all part of the game," she pointed out. Her eyes wanted to droop closed. She wasn't used to all this outdoor activity.

His arm came around her, hugging her closer and adding to the smile in her heart. "I can remember when you insisted you weren't good at games," he said quietly.

"Hey, times have changed," she said.

"Does that mean that we're ready for a charades rematch?"

"Soon," she said with a laugh. Although sometimes it seemed as if she'd been playing at charades all her life, acting out a role and hoping someone would guess right. Only no one had until Ryan. He seemed to know all the answers to her life. That ought to worry her and she promised to let it once she wasn't so tired.

Ryan looked into the back seat through the rearview mirror. "They're dead to the world," he said.

Val turned slightly to see the three sleeping children curled up behind her. She warmed at the feeling of belonging that sharing the day—and the night—with them brought. "Poor things," she said. "They look all crowded back there."

"They've always done that," he replied.

"They're growing up and getting bigger." Val turned to settle back down against his shoulder with a sleepy yawn. "Next time we go on a trip we should take my van."

"Sure," he agreed.

Suddenly she felt her heart skip a beat. Val couldn't believe what she'd said or what she'd heard. She'd mentioned a next time as if it were a sure thing and Ryan hadn't disagreed.

It all felt so comfortable, like the proverbial old pair of shoes. The kids accepted her. She could laugh with them, but also correct them. She really couldn't define when things had clicked between her and Ryan and his family. It seemed as if they'd been a part of each other's lives forever, like a family.

Family. Val tried the word on and then tottered about a bit, like a teenager trying her first pair of high-heeled shoes. She hadn't been part of a real family for a long time now. She'd almost forgotten what it was like to share one's life and to function as a unit.

Family. She let her mind wiggle around in it. It didn't fit too badly. Actually the longer she wore it the more comfortable it felt. The fears that should have rushed in seemed to have been left at the park, or at her office. The only thing nagging at her was a sense of regret, a silent shadow deep in her heart that there was something missing from her family. Someone missing.

Would any happiness ever be complete while her son was still a mystery to her?

Chapter Twelve

Grandma and Grandpa are here," Richard bellowed soon after lunch on Sunday.

"Grandma and Grandpa are here," Robert echoed.

"We heard you," Ryan said. "You guys don't have to repeat each other."

"We're not," the twins chorused.

Val's face must have worn an obvious expression of perplexity because Casey laughed and hastened to explain, "Both sets must have come together," then hurried outside.

Ryan slowly followed the kids out and Val, in turn, followed him. Both sets? Sets of what? Then the light dawned. How could she be so stupid? Sets meant Ryan's parents *and* Maggie's parents.

Val scolded herself as her stomach fluttered. What in the world had she expected? There was nothing unusual in Maggie's parents still being alive. And his wife's parents certainly had a right to see their grandchildren. Even more so now, since the children were their only link to a lost loved one. Val followed discreetly behind everybody.

Ryan's parents were both tall and on the thin side, his father closer to very thin. Val remembered Ryan saying something about a heart attack. Fortunately it had been a mild one, though the old man had had to slow down. But he still had cheerful brown eyes, which had been passed on to Ryan and the twins.

The maternal grandparents leaned a little more to husky in that grandma was short and on the plump side. Her husband spoke with such a rough growl that it was hard to believe his words got by his smiling lips.

Hugs were exchanged all around and birthday greetings bestowed upon Casey's smiling head. Each grandfather reached in his pocket and handed each boy a large coin. The boys' eyes widened.

"Oh, wow," Robert exclaimed.

"Look, Dad," Richard said.

Suddenly Ryan's eyes grew large. "A silver dollar," he exclaimed. "That's more than my weekly allowance when I was their age."

"Inflation, son," his father explained.

"Fifty cents. Fifty cents for the whole week and I had to keep the garage clean for that."

His words were so plaintively little boy that Val's lips quivered and her vision blurred. Damn. What was wrong with her lately? The stupidest things made her all weak and sentimental.

Ryan's parents advanced toward her with his in-laws following close behind. "Mom, Dad, this is Val," Ryan said, coming to stand beside her. "These are my par-

ents, Ted and Judy Crawford, and these are Bob and
Karen Maloney, Maggie's parents.''

Broad smiles greeted her and Val shook hands with
each grandparent in turn. Mrs. Maloney was last and Val
held her breath, but the woman's smile was just as broad
as the rest and her eyes were welcoming. Val scolded
herself for being nervous. It wasn't like she was trying to
replace anybody.

''We've heard so much about you,'' Mr. Crawford
said, beaming.

Val could only stare stupidly.

Mrs. Maloney sensed her uncertainty and laughed.
''Children always talk, dear.''

And just what had they said? Val wanted to ask, but
caring to know seemed too related to caring about them
all and she wasn't sure she wanted to admit how far that
emotion went.

''Let's go in,'' Casey suggested. ''So I can open my
presents.''

''Yeah,'' the boys chorused. They each had small
packages of their own. Apparently the grandparents
didn't want to leave anyone out.

Away from the watchful eyes, Val managed to relax a
bit. Ryan put his arm around her as they went inside, but
rather than make her feel self-conscious, it made her feel
a part of the family. No reason to feel awkward about
her presence.

Once inside, Val took requests for drinks and slipped
into the kitchen to pour two beers, three lemonades and
four iced teas, but was called back out only moments
later.

''Look, Val,'' Casey cried, holding up a sweater and
skirt set from Maggie's parents. ''Aren't they rad?''

"I'm not sure about that," Val said with a grin. "But they sure are pretty."

Casey made a face and opened the other gift. It held a charm bracelet, with twenty-five dollars tucked inside.

"We wanted to get you some jeans but figured we'd get the wrong size," Mr. Crawford said.

"Or the wrong designer label," his wife added.

"Thanks a bunch, everybody," Casey said, going around to hug the grandparents in turn.

"Boy, twenty-five dollars. That used to be a whole year's allowance for me," Ryan grumbled. Everyone chuckled indulgently, while Val patted his hand.

"I have the receipts if Casey wants to exchange anything," Mrs. Maloney said, looking directly at Val. "Would you like me to leave them with you?"

Val was momentarily taken aback. "Me? Well..."

"Casey said that the two of you shop together," the woman said.

Val had trouble keeping her smile. Her eyes darted to Casey, but she was helping her brothers unwrap their presents while Ryan was discussing Friday's rain with the two men.

"Yes," Val replied. "That will be fine."

She and Casey had gone shopping only once, but it had obviously made an impression. Had the trip been that exciting, or was Casey starved for female companionship? Either way, Val had a sense of pleasure that Casey had accepted her as well as she had, but what did that say about her relationship with Ryan?

"Would you put these together, please?" The boys were standing before her, holding out pieces for balsa wood gliders.

"I'll try," Val said. "But I've never assembled an airplane before."

"Bring them here, guys," Ryan said. "I'll put them together."

"Your hands are too big," Richard said. "You always mash them up."

"Well, excuse me," Ryan said, but the boys were already ignoring him and watching Val as she carefully pushed the pieces together. It wasn't really that hard and within minutes her small, deft fingers had both gliders assembled. The boys headed outside.

"Good idea, fellas," Ryan called after them. "It's a lot easier to get them stuck in a tree out there."

"Ryan," his mother said. "You're not being nice. What kind of parent are you?"

"The same kind I had?"

His mother put a frown on her face, though her eyes were laughing. "Ted," she told her husband, "I think your son might need a lesson in respect for his elders."

"He's your son," Ted said, as Val headed back to the safety of the kitchen.

The obvious love that was flowing so freely out there almost hurt. It was how she'd always dreamed families were, when she was still foolish enough to believe that such things as dreams existed. She'd grown wiser as she'd grown older, knowing that such families existed only in books and the most wild of movie fantasies. Now she'd stumbled onto a real live loving family. Did this mean she'd been wrong all these years of insisting that dreams were a waste of time? If the dream of a family could be a reality, what other dreams had she been wrongly denying?

The idea was frightening, to say the least, and she busied herself pouring the beers. She was working on the lemonade when she heard footsteps behind her.

"Do you need any help?" Mrs. Maloney asked.

Val smiled, but shook her head. "The little that's to be done is under control."

The woman took a seat at the kitchen table. "We all are so pleased with how you've helped Ryan out these past few weeks," she said.

Val was thankful that she had to make the iced tea. It gave her something to do. "I really didn't do anything other than find them a housekeeper. Mrs. Ricco is the one you ought to thank. She's—"

"We all know precisely what you've done and it has little to do with housekeeping. You've taught them all how to smile again."

Val put the pitcher down and faced the woman. "Oh, no, you've got it wrong. It's not like that. Ryan and I are just friends."

"Of course, dear." She got to her feet. "Shall I take these drinks out while you finish the others?"

She was gone before Val had found her voice. She knew she'd have to set the woman straight sometime during the day. She didn't want them all to think that she and Ryan were serious about each other—

Ryan walked into the kitchen. "Want to help me fire up the barbecue?"

She was thankful for the interruption. "Sure, just let me hand out the iced teas and I'll be right out."

A few moments later she was alone with him in the backyard.

"What do you want me to do?" she asked.

"Hold my glass and stand back."

Not exactly a taxing assignment, but she did as she was ordered, sitting on the edge of a chaise longue and watching Ryan work. He loaded up the barbecue with charcoal, then doused the briquettes with lighter fluid. She loved to watch him move. His legs were lightly covered with dark hair and his short-sleeved knit shirt accentuated his muscles. He was strength tempered with grace, a wonderful combination.

"What did you tell your parents and in-laws about me?" she asked suddenly.

Ryan struck a large wooden match and lit the fluid. He stepped back to watch. "What's there to tell?" he asked. "I just said you're a family friend."

"Oh."

"That's true, isn't it?" he asked, keeping his eye on the flame.

Val nodded. "I guess."

Satisfied that the coals were adequately fired, Ryan walked over to where she was sitting. "Casey's real happy to have you at her party."

"I'm happy to be here," Val said slowly. "At her party."

Ryan bent down to take his drink and thanked her for her help with a kiss. She would have liked to ask him for another, but voices from the house indicated that the others were coming out.

The headlights cut a path in the night before them, but the darkness quickly reclaimed the space left behind for its own. Val was clutching her legs to herself, resting her chin on her knees as she stared out into the blackness beyond. To a child the night could be scary, but even to a child there were times when the darkness brought contentment, like now.

"You do a lot of the driving," Val said. "I should be taking a turn."

Ryan shrugged. "I don't mind," he said. "Besides, it gives my hands something to do."

"Your hands something to do?" Val laughed. "Do your hands get rowdy if they don't have anything to occupy them?"

"Sometimes."

Val did not reply. His voice seemed to have a tension to it.

"Especially when I'm with you," he added.

"Oh." His voice did have a tension to it.

"To be honest about it." His voice was low and husky. "Only when I'm with you."

Now her whole body had a tension to it. The car was filled with it, hanging in the air, squeezing at her heart.

"Your parents are nice," she said, trying to defuse that electricity.

"Yeah," he agreed. "I do well at picking good people."

Val laughed. "That's what I like best about you. Your modesty."

They let the silence carry them for a few miles. The whole weekend had been very pleasant. Casey had been very effusive in her thank yous for the stuffed dog and the boys had made her feel very useful, bringing the gliders to her innumerable times for minor repairs. Ryan had said that the toys wouldn't last past dinnertime, but when she and Ryan had left, they looked in good enough shape to make at least one more flight Monday morning.

Val savored the contentment surrounding her. The weekend and everyone in it had been pleasant. Ryan, the kids, his parents, Mrs. Ricco, and especially the Maloneys.

"You also did good in picking your in-laws," Val said.

He nodded. "Yeah, I did."

"I was a little worried when I realized they were Maggie's parents."

"No need to be," he replied. "They're good people."

"Yeah, but even so." She paused a moment, wanting to choose the best words. "I'm here and their daughter isn't."

Ryan shrugged. "That's not your fault, not my fault, not anyone's fault." She nodded slightly as he paused. "It's just one of those things that happens and no one can do anything about it."

"I know," Val said. "But even if they recognize that intellectually, just seeing me could bring back some of the pain."

"I'm sure it does," Ryan replied. "And I know they still miss her, but they also know that life is for the living."

"They love their grandkids very much."

"Hey," Ryan laughed, "they recognize quality."

"It's their own blood," Val said.

Ryan was concentrating on his driving and did not reply. Val slipped back into the silence to confer with her muse. It had been so nice to be part of the family today, and not meaning just Ryan and the kids. Everyone had accepted her, treated her as if she was special to all of them also. It was like a fantasy from her youth. She had fallen into some strange world, like Alice falling into Wonderland.

The trouble was, once she started admitting that close, loving families did exist, she began to question all sorts of things. Could she really isolate her heart from caring? Could time lost be found again? Would she be satisfied with just seeing her son, or would she want to build a life with him, trying to recapture all that time they'd been apart? Could lovers really be friends?

"Want to stop by my place?"

Ryan's low baritone came charging into the far corners of her heart and dragged Val out into the outside world. She didn't mind. Val knew that if she stayed within herself too long she would easily fall prey to idle dreaming again, and right now those possibilities seemed to promise more hopes than realities.

"My babies are expecting me," she replied. "I need to feed them and clean things up."

Ryan fell into a silence and Val wondered if he was disappointed. Maybe he wasn't, but if she didn't ask she'd never know.

"It's okay with me if you stop by my place," she said. "Yin and Yang told me that it's fine with them."

"I find it hard to believe that those little bandits care about me."

"Oh, they do."

"Why?"

His tone was highly skeptical. Her heart beat a little faster and she clutched her legs tighter. She'd shied away from intimacy before, made all sorts of speeches of regret and worry about the damage it would do to their friendship, but none of that seemed important at the moment. There was a hunger in her body, an aching need to be held and caressed, to sleep in the comfort of Ryan's arms.

"They told me that two bodies provide more warmth than one body," she said lightly.

"I've noticed that myself," he said. "There was a lot of warmth, not to say heat, the last time I stayed over."

Val just smiled, letting the pleasant warmth invade her body as she leaned against Ryan's shoulder. The miles sped by and before she had time to wonder if she was in her right mind, they were in her parking lot.

While Ryan grabbed their bags, she unlocked her door. Yin and Yang were waiting, but it was fresh canned food they were demanding, not attention. In less time than it took the cats to gobble up their dinner, Val was back out in the living room where Ryan was waiting.

"What took you so long?" he sighed as she melted into his arms.

Her lips crushed into his, hungers devouring her senses and willing her hands into feverish exploring. "How long did it take me?" she whispered. Her hands were under his shirt, roaming amid the hairs of his chest.

"Years. Lifetimes. Three minutes at least." His lips lit a trail along her neck, leaving sparks on her skin that increased the raging fire in her heart.

"Poor baby," she murmured. "I missed you, too."

He swept her up in his arms then, and swept her off to paradise. The colors of her bedroom had always seemed warm, but this night they seemed to burn. Everything seemed heat and fire, the burning powers for Ryan's touch, the raging hunger to make him her own. Their lips met over and over again, sealing the promises of passion that their hands were making.

There never was another night like this. Val could think of nothing more that life could hold that could ever touch her the way Ryan's strength could. They vowed their trust and concern and then, when the fires could no longer be contained, they became one. It was magic whose sweetness stayed even as the fires exploded, then dimmed.

Val snuggled up to Ryan's warmth and fought the sleep tugging at her eyelids. She felt a part of Ryan's family, because she was a part of him. A part physically and emotionally. There was so much that bound them together that friendship no longer covered the range and depth of it.

She could feel herself slowly plunging into a soft, dark chasm of sleep where fear had no place, where dreams still did come true if she just believed hard enough. She had fallen in love with Ryan, just as she'd vowed not to. But it wasn't frightening at all. It was right and beautiful, a wonder amid life's petty pains. She was happy.

There was a pussycat's meow from the kitchen, then another. Val struggled to wakefulness, away from the velvet chains of slumber. It was past two in the morning. Ryan was sleeping peacefully. When another angry cry drifted up to the bedroom, Val grabbed her robe and got to her feet. She'd better see what was wrong before they woke up Ryan, not that she'd mind him awake. Falling back to sleep in his arms was such fun.

The kitchen turned out to be a battleground, though only a minor one. The cats had found some ribbon she'd discarded when wrapping Casey's present and were taking turns attacking it.

"Must you be so noisy?" she asked them and picked the ribbon up. It was pretty bedraggled, mostly in shreds, so Val tossed it into the garbage. "You have better things to play with than stuff you pull out of my wastebasket."

They turned up their noses at her and began to wash each other.

"Fine," she said. "I don't need you guys to curl up with anymore anyway."

It was funny to hear the words said aloud, yet not frightening either. She wasn't sure how her change of feelings would affect her relationship with Ryan, but then if she was honest with herself, her feelings had grown into love long ago. That was why she was so moody. She'd known, deep in her heart, that she was falling in love with Ryan. Now that she admitted it, there was a certain sense of peace. She turned off the kitchen light and wandered back through the living room.

She'd like to think Ryan loved her too. That the only change this would make in the relationship would be to make it better. But she knew there was certain risk in telling him. Maybe she wouldn't yet. Maybe she'd wait and pretend that nothing was different until she got a better sense of his feelings. She didn't want to think her love wasn't returned, but she was content not to press the issue until Ryan was ready. She stopped halfway up the stairs. The light on her answering machine was blinking. She'd had a call over the weekend, while she had been gone.

Val went back down into the living room and rewound the tape, then pressed the playback button.

"Miss Dennison," the voice said, filling the silence with sudden tension. "This is Ross Chambliss."

She took a deep breath as the tape played on. "I found him," the recording said. "I found your son."

"Val?"

Val spun around to see Ryan standing at the top of the stairs.

Chapter Thirteen

I'll drop off all the photos, addresses and stuff at your office Monday morning," the recorder said, Chambliss's voice filling the deadly silence of Ryan's stare. "Call me if you want the details before then." The connection broke, but the faint whine of the recorder played on.

Ryan came down a step or two. "Val?"

She swallowed hard, playing for time as she turned to switch the answering machine off. "Did I wake you? Sorry. The cats were playing around in the kitchen and—"

"Who was that on the phone?" Ryan asked, coming down another few steps.

Butterflies danced in her stomach, which was silly. Why should she be worried about telling Ryan the whole story? He already knew about her son.

"That was a private detective I hired to find my son," she said, turning back to face him.

"Why?"

"Why?" she repeated. She hadn't known what his reaction would be, but she hadn't expected that question. "Because I wanted to know where he was."

"But why?"

Ryan's voice was suddenly cold and hard as ice, causing a chill to enter her heart, and that made her angry. He had no right to be reacting this way. He should be happy for her, be sharing in her joy, not watching her with accusation in his eyes.

She lifted her chin, not in defiance exactly, but to remind herself that she was strong. "Isn't the fact that he is my son reason enough to be looking for him?"

"No." His attitude was as short and clipped as his answer, and her anger grew.

"He's my flesh and blood," she pointed out. "I gave birth to him."

"There's more to being a parent than that."

"He's still my son."

"Not legally or emotionally."

Legally? That was just man's rules for playing games. That boy had come from within her. He was her son. What did Ryan know about emotional? He was married when his children were born. Everything was nice and neat. He'd never had to lie awake at night while his arms cried out in the pain of their emptiness.

Ryan came the rest of the way down the stairs and faced her. His eyes blazed with the fire of anger, though he was visibly trying to control it. "What are you going to do now that you know where he lives?" he asked. "Are you going to drop in on him for a visit? Are you going to try to claim him?"

Val could feel that her temper was ready to explode and she bit her lip tightly for a moment. What had happened to the lover she'd had last night, to the man whose tenderness and caring had finally woken her to love?

"I don't know what I'm going to do," she said in a low voice. "I want to see him, I know that much."

"See him, like talk to him, or see him, like go to the Christmas show at his school and watch him from the audience?"

"I don't know yet," she snapped. "Mainly, I just want to be sure he's all right. That something didn't happen to his adoptive parents so that he's stuck in foster homes like I was."

Ryan nodded, his eyes softening slightly. "I can understand that, Val. But surely your detective could have learned that for you. What do you need the boy's address for?"

Why was he pushing and prodding so? It made her feel alone and under attack. "Why shouldn't I have it?" she cried. "I'm his mother."

Ryan shook his head. "A long time ago you were," he said. "I presume he has a mother now."

Ryan didn't understand at all. She'd been betrayed by love once again and that hurt worst of all. She had nothing, no one but her son. "I'll always be his mother." Her eyes burned around the edges.

"So you *are* planning on claiming him."

The idea had always been there, lying somewhere in the deep, dark shadows of her mind, and it was ready to spring to life now. Why shouldn't she want her son back? Why shouldn't she want the one person she belonged to to be with her? "I'd like him with me, yes." The accusations in Ryan's eyes burned at her and she hated him for it. "He's my son," she shouted. "I love him."

"You don't love him."

A sudden flood of anger burst the dam and tears flowed down Val's cheeks. How dare he question her love for her son! The scars on her soul from the long years of pain and emptiness were proof enough.

"Val." His voice had grown gentler but she didn't care anymore. "You love a dream. You don't know anything about the real live person that he is now."

"I don't have to." Those scars gave her strength. She was fighting to erase the guilt that had always lingered. "I love him just the way he is."

Ryan spoke quietly. "You want to snatch him away from his family. A family that loves him and that he loves in return."

"I'm his mother."

"He already has a mother. You gave him away."

Rage flared within her like a forest fire, consuming all in its path, especially the silly feeling for Ryan that she had thought was love. "Does that mean I have to pay for a mistake the rest of my life?"

"That's your choice. You can let things be or you can march in and wreck the family life he already has."

She stared at him. "That's not his real family anyway. I'm his real mother."

"Real is what a person knows. And this kid hasn't known anyone else but the parents he has right now. They're the ones who sat up with him when he had an earache, took him to his first day of school, baked him a chocolate cake for his birthday. You're not part of his life."

"I want to be."

"It's not fair to wreck what he already has just to satisfy your own selfish needs."

Selfish? To want to give her son all the love she'd been saving up for him all these years? How could Ryan not understand all that? What kind of arrogant, uncaring man was this? How in the world could she have ever thought she was falling in love with him?

"Get out," she whispered. "Get out of my home and out of my life."

"Val, think of the kid. He's a teenager, going into high school in the next year or two. Emotionally he's not in a position to have his life turned upside down."

Her anger had grown so heated, it seemed to have burned all feeling inside her. "I'll make it up to him," she said carefully. "I want to make up for everything that he's missed."

Ryan threw his hands out and grabbed her by the shoulders. "Damn it, aren't you listening?" he shouted now. "He has parents. What makes you think he's missing anything?"

"He's missing me." Her voice was cold and flat. She felt strangely numb.

"He doesn't even know you exist. How the hell can he miss you?"

She stared at him as if seeing a stranger and realizing that's what he was. Regardless of the embraces they'd shared, Ryan Crawford was a stranger. He didn't understand or care about the agonies of her past, just as he didn't understand or care about her.

"I asked you to leave," she said.

Ryan stared at her a long moment. "Have it your way," he said quietly and let go of her shoulders. Then he turned and went upstairs to finish getting dressed. A few minutes later he came back down and started toward her, but Val just turned away, staring out the window at the night. A moment later she heard the door close. The apartment was as silent as a tomb.

"I don't need him," she said to the stillness. "I don't need anyone but my son."

She wiped the traces of tears from her face and reached for the phone, not caring how late it was. She had to know more, had to wipe out the echoes of Ryan's and her argument from her mind.

Chambliss answered on the third ring. "I'm really sorry for calling this late," Val started. "But I just found your message and had to call."

"No problem," the man assured her with a weary sigh. "What do you want to know?"

Everything, she thought, but took hold of herself. "What's his name?"

"Brian Owens."

Brian. That was a good name, a strong name. A name for her to hold onto.

"He lives with a family in Houston," Chambliss went on, without waiting to be asked.

"That's where he was born."

"Yeah, his family moved around a few times because of the father's job. Made it hard to get a fix on them."

Moved around often and hard to get a fix on them. What did that mean? "What does his father do? He's not out of work is he?" Val asked. What would she do if he was? Was bad luck reason enough to lose a son? She pushed the question from her mind. "I don't mean to imply—"

The detective interrupted her. "The father's a college professor. Taught at a couple of junior colleges before moving on to a State university.

"The kid seems healthy and happy. There's two younger girls in the family, both adopted also."

"I see." Though she didn't. Her stomach seemed twisted into knots that grew tighter with the silence.

"Look, I'm sorry again about calling so late. I'll just wait until you bring the report around in the morning."

"Okay. I've got pictures of the boy, addresses, and family background. And my bill," he added. "Then I'm dropping out. What you do from here on is strictly your show."

Was he censorious or was she getting paranoid? "That will be fine," Val said coolly. "I'll wait to see you in the morning."

"Damn it," Ryan exclaimed as the oncoming car cut back into its lane. "Idiot." What the hell was that guy doing passing here?

Then Ryan fixed his attention on the broken yellow lines dividing the two lane highway. It was getting close to dusk, so vision was a little poorer, but the other driver had been within his rights to pass. The guy might have been cutting it a little short, but Ryan knew that he should have been paying better attention himself. He fixed his eyes on the road. The last thing in the world his kids needed right now was him moping and mooning like some high-school freshman and smashing into something, sending himself to kingdom come. It had been two days since his breakup with Val and he should be over it by now.

"Oh, hell," he muttered to himself and sighed. He was lucky that things had broken up before he had really gotten himself involved. He and Val had become friendly, very friendly, but it wasn't as if commitments, emotional or otherwise, had been made by either of them. No, he was lucky that this thing with her son had come out so that they realized how far apart they were on some basic issues.

Ryan shook his head. He could understand Val's pain, but she was an adult. Adults were supposed to take pain and live with it. They weren't supposed to screw up some kid's life just to make themselves happy. He couldn't believe that she could be that selfish. An evening up with the kids was just what he needed to wash her from his system.

He sighed again. Until this week, selfish was not a word that Ryan would ever have used in connection with Val Dennison. Generous, caring, loving and all their derivatives, but never selfish.

She had gotten on so well with his children. She listened and she understood them. His shoulders slumped and Ryan wished he could just find some cave and hide for a couple of lifetimes.

He pulled into the cottage drive, forcing a smile onto his face. No more mopes and gloominess. That wasn't the purpose of this trip. The kids would be really surprised to see him, he thought as he climbed out of the car. He didn't usually drive up for a visit during the week.

"Daddy!" Casey cried, running out of the house to greet him. "What are you doing here?"

Long shapely legs poked out of Casey's cutoff jeans. She was on the brink of so many firsts—her first date, her first love, her first broken heart. He'd felt quite adequate as a little girl's father, but she was no longer a little girl. He reached into the car for his overnight bag.

"Hey, I came to spend some time with my best friends," he said, forcing a laugh into his voice. "Can't blame me for being lonely without you guys, can you?"

Casey didn't join in his laughter but just peered into the car. "Where's Val?"

"She didn't come," Ryan replied as he headed toward the cottage door.

"Oh."

The air hung heavy with his daughter's concern, but he didn't want to look at her face to confirm it, so he hurried on into the house.

"Why not?" Casey followed him inside.

"Because she didn't want to," Ryan snapped. He was immediately sorry, but he wanted to end the discussion, so he busied himself getting a drink of water. "She had a lot of work to do," he added.

"You guys had an argument, didn't you?"

Her accusing eyes didn't look baby blue. They looked so adult that Ryan forced himself to look into the glass as he drank slowly.

"You ought to call her later," his daughter told him.

He spilled the remains of his glass into the sink and didn't answer or look up.

"A man *is* expected to make the first move, you know."

His glass was empty, but Ryan still didn't say anything. The receding pad of bare feet told him that Casey had left. He put the glass into the dishwasher.

His daughter had been getting close to Val, but she'd get over it, he told himself. It would be best just to leave her alone. Fortunately the boys wouldn't feel the same way as their sister. They probably wouldn't even notice Val's absence.

A slamming upstairs door and the thundering sound of their feet on the stairs signaled the approach of his sons, and Ryan turned eagerly toward the living room. The twins came rushing over to his arms.

"Hi, Dad."

"What are you doing here tonight?"

"Hi, guys. Just missed my buddies and had to come up."

"Where's Val?" they chorused.

It was going to be a long evening. Maybe he should just hide in his room. "She didn't come."

Mrs. Ricco saved him from further questions. "Mr. Crawford, what are you doing here? Have you had dinner? You should have let us know you were coming."

"Hey, you don't have to fix me anything," Ryan assured her even as she was bustling around.

"How about scrambled eggs?"

"Fine, terrific." He sat down at the kitchen table and motioned the boys to join him. "So how are things going? Having fun up here?"

"Yeah." They stared at him, two sets of identical eyes staring with the identical question. Finally Robert put it into words. "How come Val didn't come?"

Ryan sighed, fighting back the impatience. "I thought I'd come by myself for a change," he said. "It's not like she's a part of the family."

The boys exchanged glances, their meanings not lost on Ryan. "We like her," Richard said.

"Yeah, so do I," Ryan said quickly, then smiled as Mrs. Ricco delivered a plate of scrambled eggs in front of him. "Hey, this looks great. Thanks a lot."

"Want some coffee or milk?"

"Milk will be fine." By the time he'd had it, he was able to smile at the boys again. "So, guys, what do you say to a hot game of charades tonight? Or how about Trivial Pursuit?"

Robert shrugged his shoulders. "We rented *Space Invasion from Mars* for tonight."

Richard nodded. "We've been waiting weeks to see it."

Ryan's spirit sagged, but he just dug into his eggs with gusto. "Well, that sounds like fun too. It's one I've been wanting to see, too." Swell, two hours of mindless staring. Should be real effective in keeping him from thinking of Val. He might as well have brought her picture along.

"I couldn't do anything about tomorrow's luncheon," Marcie said. "They'd sold a lot of tickets based on the fact that you would be speaking."

Val nodded. It was turning out to be harder to get away than she'd expected. It wasn't just this commitment to speak at the Women in Communications meeting tomorrow. There were a million little things that needed to be done if Val was to take a few days off work. It was already Wednesday, three days since she'd heard the news, and it didn't look like she'd get down to Houston before the weekend. Not that a weekend would be easier. She'd still have to make arrangements for the office, and her cats in case she wasn't back by Monday morning.

"Get me a flight to Houston leaving sometime late Friday afternoon," Val finally said. "Let's forget about trying to make it any earlier."

Marcie scribbled in her notes. "And when do you want to return?"

Return? Who knew? It might be on the next flight out or it might be weeks, depending on what her heart decided when she saw Brian.

"Val?"

"I'm sorry." She shook her head to clear all the conflicting debris. "Leave that open for now."

"Okay," her secretary said and then quietly left.

Once the door closed, Val sighed, letting her body sag. She and Marcie had been tiptoeing around each other for the past few days and Val knew that it was all her fault. For months now she had been planning what was going to be the most joyful event of her life, finding her son. So what had gone wrong? She put her face in her hands, holding her eyes shut before the tears started spilling out again. Though there probably wasn't any moisture left, just pain.

Everything had gone completely to hell ever since Chambliss called with the news. She was doing nothing but finding fault with people. Marcie had even threatened to quit yesterday. The evenings had been especially horrible. Val's whole soul, heart and body, every part of her, wanted to be with Ryan, to have his support. She missed running her fingers through his unruly hair, and going to the concerts in the park, sitting hand in hand under the moonlight. She missed talking about anything and everything. She missed the contented silences. She especially missed lying by his side.

Even Yin and Yang seemed to be angry at her, grumbling and turning up their noses at all the special treats she offered them. It was as if they had planned something special for their evenings and she was screwing things up. Her apologies were not accepted.

Then, to make things even worse, what she had expected to be a source of solace had turned out to be a source of pain. Chambliss had brought the material on her son Monday morning. Scurrying to the privacy of her office, she'd locked the door behind her, wanting no interruptions while she looked at her son's picture. Eagerly, she'd torn the package open.

There had been a number of pictures in the packet and Val had pawed through them until she'd found a head shot. Chambliss must either have gotten close or used a telephoto lens, because he had gotten a good full-face shot of a smiling teenage boy. Val had let her eyes feast on the picture and waited.

And waited some more. But there had been no outpouring of emotion, no tears of joy. There had still been excitement, but that original feeling had been joined by disappointment. What she'd held had been nice pictures of a good-looking teenage kid, but not somebody she had known. It had been ridiculous to feel surprised at that thought because she really didn't know him. But she had felt as if she ought to.

Val had spent the next few days going through the packet of information again and again. Her son's name was Brian Owens. He was a very good student, a good wrestler and an average baseball player. The father was a college professor and the mother was an elementary school teacher who worked part-time as a substitute. The two other children in the family that Chambliss had mentioned were two girls, one ten years old and the other six. In addition to birds and goldfish, the family had two dogs and one cat. Each time she'd read the papers she'd felt slightly guilty for spying on the personal lives of these people, so she'd pushed them aside, going back to the pictures.

Val pulled the photos over again now as she had so many times these past few days. She stared again at Brian's face, but still she could find no telltale features that reminded her of herself or her own mother and father. She didn't see any similarity at all to her, and found just a faint resemblance to Danny.

Her intercom buzzer sounded and Val pushed the pictures back into her drawer.

"You have a visitor," Marcie announced.

Visitor? Val glanced at her calendar, but before she could say anything her secretary announced that she was sending the visitor in. The door opened slowly and Casey shyly eased in.

"Casey." Val got up and rushed over to meet the girl, giving her a big hug that was returned with interest. "I'm so happy to see you."

"I'm happy to see you too," Casey said.

There was a moment of awkward silence, which Val rushed in to fill. "Sit down, please." She led her to a chair. "Would you like anything to drink? Soda, milk, iced tea?"

"No, thank you," Casey replied, shaking her head. "The boys are in town for a dental checkup and I only have a short time."

"Okay." Val nodded and wondered how else to fill the silence. She walked around her desk to sit in her own chair.

Casey leaned forward slightly, her hands primly folded in her lap. "Daddy's real down," she said. "I mean like, in the dumps."

"I'm sorry to hear that."

"What happened?" the girl asked, wide, honest blue eyes peering straight into Val's soul.

Val squirmed. If Ryan hadn't told the girl, Val wasn't certain she ought to. "We're not compatible," she said, falling into an adult brush-off.

Frown lines creased Casey's smooth forehead. "You guys looked real compatible to me, especially under the lilac bush."

Val cleared her throat. Apparently adult brush-offs didn't work with teenagers. "There's all kinds of areas of compatibility," she said. "And we just happened to go into a new area and . . . and sparks came out."

"In what?" Casey's voice was so earnest and full of concern.

Val just shook her head, suddenly not wanting to lie to the girl, but not wanting to tell it all again either. "It's a long story, honey."

"I got time."

Val was momentarily tempted to point out that Casey had said she didn't have time enough for a drink, but she had no spirit for any kind of repartee. And before she knew it, the whole story was flowing out, like a river through a broken dam. Val didn't leave anything out, especially her hurt at Ryan's reaction to her wanting to meet the son she'd given up so long ago.

After Val had finished her story, there was a long moment of silence as Casey just stared at the floor. Val's stomach was troubled. Maybe she shouldn't have told the girl all that. After all, Casey was on the way to womanhood, but she really was still a child.

Finally the girl looked up, her eyes burdened with a terrible pain. "It's all my fault."

"Casey," Val exclaimed as she hurried around to sit in the other guest chair. She took Casey's hands in her own, holding them tightly. "It has nothing to do with you."

"Yes, it does," the girl insisted, squirming slightly and blinking away the wateriness in her eyes. "You see, I'm adopted."

"Oh." Val could feel her hands beginning to shake and she tightened her hold on Casey. "I didn't know that."

"Not too many people do." Casey screwed her face into tight earnestness and went on. "It's not like we don't want to tell anybody. It's just that we don't talk about it." She shrugged and looked around the office.

"Daddy always says family is family and it doesn't matter how you get in. Once you're in, you're family forever."

"Nothing's forever," Val murmured against the pain in her heart.

But Casey ignored Val's comment and went right on. "There are two ways to get into a family, be born in one or get adopted. But once you're in, it's all the same, he says. They got to invite you to the weddings and funerals and they've got to leave your picture in the family albums."

The shakiness moved up from her hands into her lips and Val found her breathing coming a little faster. "Sounds like you and your father have discussed this subject a great deal."

"Not that much," Casey replied. Her eyes stared off into space at some distant time. "Just when I was in fifth grade."

Fifth grade? "Is that when you started wondering who your real parents are?"

Casey shook her head, bringing her gaze back to Val's. "I've always known who my real parents were. Ryan and Maggie Crawford," she said with a strange defiance in her voice, a protective strength. "They were the ones who took care of me all the time."

Val felt like a knife had pierced her heart, but she just swallowed hard and clenched her jaw. "I see. Why fifth grade, then?"

"A new girl moved in just down the street when I started fifth grade. We got to be friends. Then she told me she was adopted and we became special friends. And on spring break we were going to go on a Girl Scout camping trip together. We planned it for weeks."

Val felt a sense of apprehension as Casey paused, apparently because she had to. The girls eyes were pooling and her lips wanted to quiver.

"Then her birth mother came and took her away."

"And the two of you didn't get to go on your camping trip," Val finished for her. "I imagine you were very upset."

"I was terrified," Casey said, anger joining to dance with the other emotions on her face. "I was scared to death that *my* birth mother was going to come and take me away."

Val tried to fight the shadows of despair trying to crowd into her heart. "There was probably no reason for you to be afraid," she said. "I presume the other girl's adoption wasn't finalized."

But her son's adoption was complete, and wasn't she hoping, in the furthest, secret corners of her heart, to bring him back with her?

Casey shook her head. "She wasn't really adopted," she said. "She was a foster child and just said she was adopted."

Val felt herself sinking into an emotional quagmire. With her own experiences as a child, she could understand the other girl trying to tell herself—and others— that she was really adopted, that she really belonged to somebody.

"Mom and Dad spent a lot of time explaining the difference between adoption and foster care to me," Casey went on. "But it took me a long time to get over being scared. I had nightmares for a long time after that."

Val felt the whirlpool trying to drag her into the darkness of despair. She fought and struggled, trying to swim toward a ray of light. She didn't want to hear, didn't need to hear, this.

"But now that you're older," Val said, "I'm sure that you'd like to know who your—" she paused, swallowed and took a deep breath "—birth mother is."

"Not really," Casey said slowly, faint traces of fear showing in the girl's eyes. "Not yet. It's still scary to think about."

"But you're older now," Val protested, fighting to keep anger from creeping into her voice. Someone had to understand how she felt.

"But not old enough." Casey's voice had risen from emotions and Val swallowed her fears. She forced her hold on Casey's hands to be reassuring.

"It's okay, honey," Val said.

Casey swallowed hard. "You see, I'm just starting to understand how to use makeup and next year I have to go to high school," she said. "Before I know it, I'm going to have to be taking care of myself and I don't even know what I want to do yet. I wouldn't know what to say to a mother I didn't know."

The child part of the woman-child before Val had taken center stage, frightened and needing care. Val felt defeated. What could she say that would take the fear from Casey's eyes and make her understand? What could she say that would take the sick feeling away from her own stomach?

"Sometimes I wonder about my birth mother," Casey admitted, her shoulders slumping. "I wonder if she's happy, or if she's sick or homeless. If she's lonely. I mainly wonder why she gave me up for adoption. You know, did she think I was a bother or real ugly or something like that?"

Val looked down at their hands so tightly clutching each other's and clenched her teeth as the silence screamed in her ears. "I'm sure it wasn't any of those things," she said softly. "Mothers love their children, even those they can't keep for some reason. And all babies are beautiful."

Casey shook her head, a faint grin struggling to live on her lips. "The twins weren't. They were all red and screaming all the time." Her grin faded and her eyes took on that faraway look again. "I was really jealous of them when they were born. I was too young to be worried that now that Mom and Dad had finally had children of their own they wouldn't want me, but I was upset because the twins had brown hair just like Mom and Dad. I was the only redhead and felt really out of things."

"You have beautiful hair," Val told her, and Casey's familiar grin again surfaced for a moment.

"But that's not the real issue, is it?" she said. "We were talking about my birth mother and would I want to meet her. When I'm older I probably would." Casey paused and shrugged. "Yes, I know I would, but I don't want to be all mixed up when that happens. I want to be a grown-up person. All finished and . . . and not scared of a whole bunch of stuff. You know what I mean?"

Val just nodded and didn't trust herself to speak. Afraid that if she freed her tongue all the secrets of adulthood would come spilling out. Not the good magic secrets, but the dark secrets that no one wanted to talk about. The fact that uncertainties and fears walked with you all your natural life. And maybe beyond.

"Being a kid is really scary," Casey said. "You know, nothing is safe, nothing is certain. Your whole world is based on your parents and if something should happen to them, what do you have left?''

Val knew the answer to that one only too well, but Casey gave her no time to answer, even supposing she wanted to.

''I have a friend whose parents are getting divorced and she's so scared. She doesn't know who she'll be living with or where she'll be going to school. Her mom's getting an apartment so she might not be able to keep her dog. She's doing terrible in school because she can't think straight anymore.''

Casey's voice suddenly died down and silence reigned for a moment. ''I'm glad you came,'' Val said, though her heavy heart was even heavier now.

Casey got to her feet slowly. ''Please don't stay mad at Daddy,'' she said. ''He really is miserable without you.''

''I'm not certain it's up to me,'' Val told the girl. ''I'm miserable without him, but some things aren't so easily mended.''

Casey nodded and walked toward the door. ''Well, I'd better get downstairs to meet Mrs. Ricco. I promised I wouldn't make them wait.''

''I'm sure she would understand,'' Val assured her.

''She's a nice lady,'' Casey agreed.

Val followed her to the door and they both stood staring at each other. She wanted to hug the girl, but what did Casey want? Val wasn't sure about anything anymore. They settled on shaking hands.

''Are you going to come out and see us again?'' Casey asked.

Val shrugged. ''I don't know.''

''Okay.'' The voice was tremulous with a good dose of forced cheerful. ''Maybe when you're not so busy.''

There was no way she could trust her voice, so Val just nodded. Casey looked at her, then the girl flung her arms around Val for a brief, precious moment before hurrying out the door. Quick, silent tears overflowed Val's eyes as she turned back to her desk. Was she going to be the ogre when she came into her son's life? Would he reject her, angry at his abandonment years ago and fearful of the disruption in his life?

Val took a deep breath. Her case was different. And maybe Casey would feel differently if her birth mother did appear. Casey had admitted to having questions she would like to ask the woman. Everything would be fine, Val told herself. All she had to do was keep repeating it all the way to Texas. Then maybe she'd believe it.

Chapter Fourteen

Saturday morning found Val sitting in her rental car and glumly staring down the Houston street. It was a pleasant street of single-family homes. Most of those homes seemed filled with children. If Brian came to live with her, would she have to move out of her town house? Didn't boys need a yard to play in?

Val ran her fingers through her hair, her irritation level rising. That was stupid. Boys grew up everywhere, from apartments to farms. She let her arm flop down onto the steering wheel.

She'd forgotten how warm it was in Houston in the middle of July. The lake with its cool breezes, sparkling water and Ryan came into her thoughts. That's where she ought to be, a little voice told her. With Ryan and the kids, not here playing secret agent. Val closed her eyes against the thoughts.

Was that what she was doing here, playing secret agent? Just what was she going to do? Snatch Brian when he stepped outside his house? From the physical description that Chambliss had given her, the boy was already as big as she was.

"This is stupid," she muttered as she turned the ignition. "I'd better get out of here before someone reports a suspicious-looking woman to the police."

If she really wanted to regain custody of her son, she needed to get a lawyer on the job and go about it in a civilized manner. A tiny voice asked what was so civilized about snatching a child from the only home he had ever known, but Val concentrated on checking for traffic and refused to listen.

Suddenly the door of Brian's house opened and people came out. The parents came out first, talking as they headed toward the station wagon parked in the driveway. Two girls bounced along behind them, a blonde and a dark brunette. Then Brian stepped out dressed in a baseball uniform. Val's heart wanted to stop. She wanted to run over to look at him closer, to hug and hold him, to run away and never chance the look of anger that might come to his eyes when he learned who she was.

The family got into the car, which backed out into the street, then headed west. They're probably going to one of Brian's baseball games, Val thought with a shrug. Her car was already pointed in that direction, so she might as well go along. The rationalization was easy. Her heart raced as if she was running the whole way.

The park turned out to be fairly close to their home. Traffic was light, so Val never had to worry about losing them. She followed them into the parking lot but parked her car well on the opposite side of the lot.

She swallowed hard and watched as Brian was greeted vigorously by all his teammates. Apparently he was popular. Since Chambliss's report said he was only an average player, his popularity must be due to his personality. He must be a nice kid, a good friend to others. Pride tried to rear its head, but painful uncertainty beat it down. She'd never been popular as a child and she was always the last one picked for any junior hi gym team. Who had helped him grow with confidence and friendliness in his heart? a little voice asked. It didn't matter, Val assured herself. She was just glad her child wasn't suffering from uncertainties the way she had.

Val's eyes misted over and she turned them back toward the Owens family. The parents looked like nice solid folk, dressed informally and talking easily with the other parents. The youngest child was holding a doll and staying close to her parents, while the middle child shagged balls for her brother's team. One looked like a tomboy and the other was already a little lady, same family, yet so different.

Suddenly Val found herself almost staring intently at the youngest. Unlike her blond sister she had very dark hair and her eyes looked somewhat different. Slowly Val edged closer and cast furtive glances at the child, who stared at her shyly and smiled. Up close Val saw that the girl had faintly Oriental features. She was so pretty.

A nagging little voice screeched at her. Would her trying to take Brian make *all* the children afraid? Would they all have nightmares the way Casey had? Val walked hurriedly away from the family, taking a seat far out at the end of the bleachers, away from the batter's box, away from where she guessed most of the people would sit. When the players filed onto the field, Val breathed a sigh of relief to see that her choice left her where she wanted to be, alone.

Val concentrated on her son. He hit the ball about half the times he was at bat and he played somewhere in the back, outfield, she thought.

His movements on the playing field weren't awkward though. He hadn't inherited her gawkishness but rather the physical grace and talent of his birth father, the college quarterback. The term "birth parent" no longer caused her any distaste. It would be a part of their lives from now on.

By the second half of the last inning, Val became more and more caught up in the game. Brian's team was ahead six to five. The opposing team was at bat and two men were out, two on base, when another boy came to bat. Judging from the cheers of the crowd and his teammates, the kid was a good player. He hit the ball high, but Brian came under it, and the crowd hushed. When Brian caught the ball, cheers broke loose. His teammates charged him, his parents clapped and smiled, his little sisters jumped up and down, screaming. Val felt happy and wanted to cry at the same time. She wanted to tell everyone that that was her son who had caught that ball, that her son had won the game for his team, but she just kept silent. Her joy was too great to be shared with strangers.

After a few moments, the cheering stopped and the boys gathered up their equipment while the parents drifted toward the parking lot. Another set of teams was coming on to play, but Val just sat there and stared. She had expected to feel happiness at seeing her son, but she hadn't expected to feel such pride in his achievements, such a deep, earth-shattering love for him. It was like nothing she'd ever felt before. A little voice tried to mock her, to remind her of a love that had been different, but just as deep if not deeper than what she felt for that boy who was a virtual stranger to her. But she just turned her head and her heart from the voice.

Suddenly her heart took a jump. Brian was coming her way. Her son was going to pass right by her. Val swallowed her fear and stood up. She put herself right in the boy's path.

"Nice catch," Val said.

He stopped, blinking once in surprise. Val looked into his cool level gaze and felt as if she were looking in a mirror. She had given him something. At least physically.

"Thank you, ma'am," he murmured politely and then, stepping around her, went to join his family.

"Good game," the mother said.

"Good concentration," the father said. "All that backyard practice finally paid off."

"You were great," the youngest girl said as she hugged him around the waist.

"Way to go, big bubba," the middle girl snickered. "You didn't drop the ball or do anything else stupid."

"Shut up, twerp," Brian returned, trying to fit a frown to his face but not succeeding.

He stood comfortably, face flushed, basking in the warmth of his family, just as Casey had radiated the love of her family on her birthday. The love of the parents in both cases, the people who had cared for Brian and Casey since they were babies, was obviously unconditional. The twins adored Casey, and Brian's youngest sister adored him, and so did his middle sister though he probably fought with her constantly.

Suddenly Val saw all sorts of resemblances. Not between her and Brian, but between him and his family.

Their smiles were the same, all gentle and understanding. Their eyes all reflected generosity and tolerance. Their open friendliness seemed to embrace all who were around them. She had given him life years ago, but they had sustained that life. They'd given him love and made him into the young man he was. He wasn't hers anymore.

Val could feel the tears coming down and she turned away. By the time she neared the car, she was running, but she managed to pull out of the parking lot and get part way down the street before her sobbing began in earnest.

Val sat in a small booth at the back of the coffee shop and stared out the window into the Houston evening. She had a half cup of coffee and a partially eaten banana cream pie in front of her and a full load of bone-tired exhaustion riding her shoulders. This had been one hell of a day. She'd been on a roller coaster ever since receiving that call from Chambliss. A roller coaster steeper than any she'd ever attempted and no one by her side to hold her hand. Her hand physically hurt wishing Ryan were there to hold it.

"More coffee, ma'am?"

Val peeked out of her deep hole of depression and smiled at the young waitress's soft Texas drawl. She hadn't heard one done so well for a long time and it was like a soothing balm on her soul. Not trusting herself to speak, Val just shook her head.

"Something wrong with the pie, ma'am?"

Val looked at the barely dented remains and shook her head.

"Are you all right, ma'am?" Bright blue eyes that were more suited to laughing and joking were now framed in concern.

"I have a lot on my mind." Val was surprised at how husky her voice sounded, but was pleased to see words come out without stumbling over tears. "Lot of things to sort out."

"Sometimes life deals you a full hand."

Concern turned to sympathy in the young woman's youthful, almost unlined face, but Val could see edges of pain in the corners of her eyes. Few people escaped life unscarred and most were better for the experience.

"You're not making much money off the space I'm occupying," Val said. She was happy to see that her voice sounded almost normal. "I probably should order something or leave."

The woman laughed and brought youthful joy back into her eyes. "Ain't exactly got hordes of people a-hankering for that space," she said with a laugh.

Val smiled with her as she looked around at the less than half-full dining area.

"We're really hopping at lunch," the waitress said. "And then again from ten to midnight, and reasonable at breakfast. In between it's stragglers."

Val nodded.

"So if you're hungry I'll be glad to get you something, but if you ain't, don't push it."

"Thank you," Val murmured.

"If you want anything, just give a holler. I'll be around."

Val tried to smile but gave up the attempt when the waitress was no longer looking, just rubbing her eyes and **sighing.** Chambliss's call had sent her straight to cloud nine, from which Ryan had quickly brought her down.

The next few days she'd lived with the pain of what her loss had been and fear of the unknown. Once she'd gotten to Houston that fear had turned into plain old bone-chilling scared.

After seeing the Owens's house and neighborhood Val had almost had herself under control. She had been all set to go to a lawyer and start proceedings to recover Brian for herself, but then Brian had come out and she'd followed the family to his baseball game.

Val had fallen from that hodgepodge of emotions and was now lying wounded and uncertain. All of her dreams were now in question, in jeopardy, and she no longer felt she knew who she was or what she wanted. All she knew was that although Brian was her birth son, he was not her real son. Not by Casey's definition, not by Val's own heart's definition.

Brian lived in a house of love. His parents loved him, his sisters loved him, each in her own way, and he loved them in return. That was all very obvious in the touching, the shared looks, the inside humorisms. She had no part in any of that. She hadn't nurtured that love or fostered it. She hadn't done a damn thing but allow her body to give him life until he could maintain it on his own.

No, it hadn't been on his own, just without her. She'd carried him for nine months. That didn't give her many rights. Not compared with fourteen years.

Val closed her eyes. In many ways, the Owens household reminded her of the Crawford household. A household of which she had been a part. A household that had wrapped her in its collective arms. A wry smile twisted her lips. Her blood was here, where she was an outsider. In the Crawford household, where there was none of her flesh and blood, she was accepted.

Now she knew without a doubt where Brian belonged. He belonged with his family, he belonged at
home, he belonged with the people who had nurtured
and cared for him. He belonged with the Owenses who
were about to guide him on those last fateful miles into
adulthood.

That decision hurt badly, but the main advantage was
that *she* was the only one who hurt. No one else's life
was uprooted. Brian had sunk his roots, and as a teenager, he was no longer a sapling that could be easily
transplanted. If uprooted, he might not take to his new
environment. If a storm uprooted him, as one had her
as a child, he might sink his roots in his new environment—her environment—and grow big and strong, but
he might not. Val didn't want to be the storm that uprooted him. If his situation had been poor or intolera-
ble, that would have been different, but it wasn't. Brian's
situation was good. He was where he belonged and she
knew that.

She picked up her coffee to stifle the ache in her heart,
but the coffee cup felt cold. The liquid had the color and
cruddy film covering of stagnant swamp water. She put
it back down.

"Want a new cup?" The waitress had appeared,
smiling, at her side.

Val shook her head. "I'm full to the top and ought to
be on my way soon."

"Okay." The waitress's voice was soft and quiet. She
put the check, facedown, next to Val. "Ya'll come back
now."

Val picked up the check and looked at the pitiful remains of her snack. It was somehow a reminder of what
she'd done with her life. Started out with something

good and sweet, the affection of Ryan and his family, and mangled it so that she now had nothing.

She got to her feet and trudged over to the cashier. All she'd ever wanted was someone who would belong to her, someone to share the ups and downs of life. Now she had no one but her cats. Bought friendship.

The heaviness of her heart wanted to overwhelm her, but little scenes kept popping up in her mind like slides on a screen: Casey saying Ryan was miserable without her. Ryan saying family was those who nurtured and cared for you, not ones who shared your blood. Casey quoting Ryan in saying once you were family, you were always family and they had to let you come back home. Had she been family? Would they let her come home again? There was only one way to find out.

Chapter Fifteen

Val was tired as she drove to the airport, but it was a comfortable kind of tired that was free of pain. She'd made her decisions and put her life in order. The decisions and results weren't great, but they were the best available for everyone concerned. And Brian Owens wouldn't be hurt at all.

He was her son, but at least for a while, she thought it would be best to think of him as Brian Owens. Brian Owens growing into manhood in a complete family, with parents, siblings, grandparents and cousins. Even in that kind of family there were a lot of things that Brian Owens would have to come to terms with. He didn't need the problem of two women, one who had borne him and another who had given him his life, fighting for his attention.

Maybe if she was lucky, there would be time enough for her later, when he was a man. Then maybe Val could have a small piece of him to know and love.

What she wanted most right now was what she'd had before Chambliss's call. She wanted Ryan Crawford to herself. She wanted to lie by his side and have him soothe all her lingering hurts. She wanted to give completely of herself like she had done before, for in that giving she was enriched and fully alive.

Her son would always live in her heart and there would be times that she would miss him very, very much. There would be times when her heart would ache and she would wonder how he was doing and how life was treating him. But her life was with Ryan and his family right now, and when those dark times tried to take over her soul, with luck the Crawfords would be there to help her fight them back.

Life was a mosaic of twists and turns, yet at times it looked as if there were a grand plan that tied it all together. Years ago she'd cast her son upon the waters and he'd floated right into the heart of a woman who needed a child to love. And now, when she needed someone to love, the gods gave her Ryan Crawford and his motherless brood. What you lost on the slides you made up on the merry-go-round.

Val parked her rental car in an open slot and hurried to check the car in. Ryan Crawford was who Val needed to make her life complete. The kids were a marvelous bonus. Oh, God, she prayed, please don't let me be too late. She'd thrown out some foolish words and made some stupid choices in the past few days. She hoped that she wouldn't need to spend the rest of her life regretting it.

"I'd like a seat on your earliest flight to Fort Wayne, Indiana, please." Breathless from almost running, Val paused to catch her breath.

The reservation clerk keyed into his machine. "That would be flight 364, leaving Houston tomorrow at 1:10 in the afternoon, with a connecting flight out of Chicago."

"Tomorrow?" Val knew her mouth was hanging open, but she was aghast. Tomorrow? They expected her to wait until tomorrow to see Ryan? "But . . . but," she stammered. "I have to get home."

"I'm sorry, ma'am, but—"

"Okay, get me to Chicago. I'll find something from there myself."

"I can't, ma'am, there's—"

"How about Detroit?"

He shook his head.

"Cincinnati. Toledo. If I have to, I can drive to Fort Wayne from any of those cities."

"Ma'am—"

"Damn it," Val snapped, slamming her fist on the counter, as her executive persona came to the fore. "I want to get home. Now get me there."

"Ma'am." The reservation clerk was extreme in his patience. "I can't. There's a huge thunderstorm covering the midwest."

Her heart fell. She could shout down a reservation clerk, but not nature. "Thunderstorm?"

"Yes." He moderated his voice slightly, apparently happy that he had her attention. "It stretches from Kansas City to just east of Cleveland. It's north of Milwaukee and south of Nashville."

Val could only blink in reply.

"Nothing's getting in," the clerk said. "I'm sorry."

The energy left her body like the gas out of a pricked balloon. "I'm sorry," she said.

"No problem, ma'am," he said, returning to his professional amiability. "Would you like me to book you on tomorrow's flight?"

Val nodded dumbly and the man's nimble fingers went to work. She handed him her ticket for updating. "There you are, ma'am," he said with a wide smile. "You are now confirmed on—"

"Thank you," Val murmured as she snatched her ticket. She knew that she was exceeding her impolite quota, but she just wanted to run and hide.

Her feet took her to the passenger waiting area and she paused to find a seat. Dumb. All that brouhaha with the reservation clerk was just plain dumb. She should have noticed herself how crowded the airport was. And all she had to do was look at the tote board and see all the canceled flights. The poor man.

All the seats in the waiting area appeared to be taken, but a phone opened up and Val rushed to it. It was evening back home. She'd give Ryan a call. It wasn't as good as seeing him in person, but it was better than nothing.

She dialed his number and the phone rang and rang, but no one answered. There was a lot of static on the line. Maybe they weren't getting through, she thought with a ray of hope lighting her heart. Val called the operator and asked her to dial. Again it rang and rang. The woman assured Val that the signal was getting through. The problem was that no one was answering the phone. Val hung up.

What was she thinking of? It was Saturday. Ryan would be up at the cottage. The phone was soon ringing there and Val clenched her free hand. Oh, please, let him be in.

"Hello." Static crackled over the lines. "Hello."

"Hello," Val said loudly. "This is Val Dennison. Who am I speaking to?"

"Hi, Val. This is Casey. How come you're yelling?"

Embarrassed, Val dropped her voice a few decibels. "I'm sorry. There's a lot of static on the line and I was afraid you wouldn't hear me."

"I don't hear any static," Casey said. "And I hear you fine."

Must be just on her end, Val thought. "How's the weather?" she asked.

"Weather?" The girl's voice turned hesitant.

Val wondered if she was going crazy or just sounded like that to everyone. "Yes," Val said. "Is it storming badly?"

"Not too bad," Casey replied. "It's raining a lot, with some thunder and lightning, but it's not real bad."

"The Houston weather people say most of the airports in the midwest are shut down because of storms."

"Oh, yeah?"

They shared a long silence, each touching lightly around the other.

"How is Houston?" Casey finally asked.

"Fine."

The girl cleared her throat. "Did you see him?"

Val knew the him that Casey was referring to, but she still took a moment of silence to gather her thoughts. "Yes, I did," she said. "But just at a distance."

"Oh."

Val didn't let the silence develop into anything. "He has a very nice family."

"That's good." Casey's voice was still uncertain.

"There's his mother, father, and two little sisters."

"Sounds nice."

"I saw them all," Val said. "But I didn't meet anybody. I'm not going to."

Casey sighed as if she'd been holding her breath. Val knew the girl was relieved, but Val wasn't up to hearing that, not just yet.

"Is your father there?" Val asked.

"No, he's on a business trip."

Val's heart sank. On a weekend? But, "Oh", was all Val said.

"Do you want me to find out where he went?" Casey asked. "Mrs. Ricco probably knows. Or I could call Grandma and Grandpa, then call you back."

"No, that's okay," Val replied. "I'll see him when I get in." Whenever that would be.

"It wouldn't take me long," Casey said. The girl's voice almost sounded pleading.

"No, really. Don't bother," Val said. "I'll see you guys when I get back."

She let the receiver fall and somehow it found the hook of its own accord. Had she screwed things up again? Why wasn't Ryan with the kids? She could run a business fine, but she wasn't worth anything when it came to her personal life.

The terminal was still crowded and it seemed that every seat and bar stool in the place had a line waiting to get it. Her tired feet dragged her around the area. Was it too late to get her hotel room back? She hailed a cab and slouched back in the seat, kicking her heels off.

She paid the cabdriver and walked into the lobby carrying her shoes and overnight bag. Val knew that walking on the sidewalk would ruin her hose but didn't really care. After all, she had probably ruined the rest of her life, so why not do in a pair of hose and complete the job? Head down, she made her way toward the desk.

"Val?" A rumpled figure appeared at her side, carrying a huge black-and-white stuffed cat.

"Ryan?" She stared from him to the cat in his arms. "What are you doing here?"

"Your secretary told me where you were staying," he said. "Val, please, I need to talk to you."

Her pain and weariness washed away like road dust during a summer storm but, strangely, as the load lifted off her shoulders her legs grew weaker.

"I'm sorry for everything that happened," he said softly. "I've never had to make the decisions you've had to make and I had no right trying to impress my opinion on you."

Val tried to smile, tried to laugh, loving every single curl in the mop that tumbled all over his head, but all she could do was cry. Slow, single tears trickled down her cheeks.

"I don't know what I'd do if I had a son I gave up at birth and hadn't seen since," Ryan said. "But it's your decision and you have a right to make it any way that you want."

"Oh, Ryan." Val didn't want to talk anymore. She just wanted to snuggle into his arms. "I saw him. I saw his family."

Ryan looked at her, his eyes loving. Fear seemed nested deep in the recesses, but mostly she saw trust and love. She paused and took a deep breath. A slight lump came up in her throat, but Val quickly vanquished it.

"I'm going to leave things be," she said. "He has a good family. He's secure. And, as you well know, security is what a teenager needs."

Ryan's hands found hers, closing tightly around them as the cat slipped sideways. "I did some research. There are organizations that will let him know you're around. That is, when he's older."

Val swallowed the tears that kept wanting to fall. "That's nice."

"You can even keep an eye on him. You know, just in case something happens."

Val nodded. "I'm sure Chambliss could do that."

"You can also help pay for his college if you want." Ryan pulled a wrinkled paper from his pocket. "I looked up some legal firms in the area. They can take care of everything. Set up a trust fund. Confidentially, of course."

This was all wonderful, reassuring even. She could be there if her son needed her, just as Ryan was here now when she needed him. Why was he? Was it out of concern that she was going to disrupt Brian's life or was there another reason?

"Ryan?"

He looked up from the paper he'd been reading from.

"What are you doing with that cat?" It wasn't what she'd meant to ask at all, but the silly thing was grinning at her, taking possession of her thoughts.

Ryan grinned, too, as he held the cat up. "It's Felix the Cat," he said. His grin slipped slightly as he pushed the cat into her arms. "I got him for you."

She took the toy, clinging foolishly to its softness, but her eyes stayed on Ryan. "Why?" she asked.

He shrugged. "The kids keep pushing for that rematch of charades," he said. "And I figured you needed some tutoring before then."

"I see." Her throat seemed unaccountably dry. "So it's because you don't want to disappoint the kids."

"Do you?"

She shook her head quickly. "Oh no, of course not. I really enjoy being with them."

The silence fell again, heavy and oppressive. This was getting them nowhere fast. She took a deep breath and plunged ahead. Her heart had been overjoyed at seeing Ryan here, but now doubts were eating at her.

"Yin and Yang would like to meet the kids," she said.

He frowned. "They tell you that?"

"Sure." She swallowed hard and went on. "They know you already and know how comfy you are to sleep against, but they're curious about the kids. You know, will the kids sneak them treats and play with them?"

"Is that important?" Ryan asked.

Val nodded. "Well, those cats are my only family," she said with a smile and an almost paralyzing attack of the jitters. "And you guys seem almost like my family, so I thought maybe we ought to all meet each other. These past few days have shaken the hell out of me and I'm afraid I'm going to need all you guys pretty badly for a while."

A couple hurrying up to the reservation desk bumped into Val slightly, and Ryan took her by the hand over to a secluded sitting area. "We're here whenever you need us," Ryan told her once they were seated. "Both me and the kids. You should know that. That's what friends are for."

"I'm afraid that 'whenever' might be pretty often and for a pretty long time," Val said with a tight smile, her hands and heart aquiver. Control had always been her byword. That was all she said she wanted, control of her life, and here she was about to risk everything on a wild gamble. "I was sort of hoping that maybe I could stay with you guys for a while."

Her courage deserted her along with the words and she stared down at their hands, clutching each other's with desperation.

"I see," was all Ryan said, his voice not saying anything more than the words.

When she dared a glance upward, he too was staring down at their hands. Her heart sank. She'd gambled and lost.

"It's not that I don't want to be there for you," he said slowly. "It's just that the kids might not understand if you just moved in for a while—"

"Sure, that's fine." Control was vital now, control so that she didn't break down in front of him. Val got to her feet. "It was just a thought. Doesn't matter though and—"

He pulled her back down to the sofa. "And I would keep forgetting," he said. "If you want to stay with us, it can't be for just a while. It's got to be forever and it's got to be legal."

Val's heart stopped. Was he saying what she thought he was saying? Her eyes met his, but she couldn't speak to save her life.

"I know I broke all our rules," he said. "And if you're angry with me, fine. But the kids don't understand all these silly games adults try to play, and that's all those rules were, part of a silly game."

Val found her voice. "And I told you right in the beginning that I was no good at games." His eyes took on a puzzled look and she smiled. Her heart was beating again, racing even, with happiness. "Don't you remember when we played charades and I warned you I was no good at games? Well, I goofed up this one pretty good too."

"Val?"

She grinned. "Looks like we both lost. Or did we both win?"

She let Felix the Cat fall to the floor at her feet and moved into his arms because there was no staying away any longer. She came back to her heaven and felt all the pain and worries of the past few days fade away. Then Ryan's lips met hers in a promise of love and devotion that shook her heart to its very core. She clung to him, wishing the moment could go on and on, but eventually the need to breathe forced them apart.

"Now, let me get this right," Ryan said slowly. "Are you saying—"

"I'm saying that I love you," she whispered, gazing up into his eyes. "And that I would like nothing better than to move into your home legally forever."

"I think I've loved you since you came into my house that first day and let the kids buffalo you into playing charades. You brought such calm, such peace, with you. I didn't want to let you go. I just didn't realize that was love until we had that fight early Monday morning. Without you all the chaos was back in my life."

She picked Felix up and sat him in her lap. "So tell me, how much tutoring were you planning on before we play charades again? Should we get started on it immediately?"

He stood up, pulling her to her feet. "The hell with Felix. I've got better ideas of what we can do with our time. I've got a very nice room upstairs with a very nice bottle of champagne on ice, just in case a very nice lady I know could be persuaded to forgive me."

"Goodness," she teased, her heart soaring above the heavens. "That certainly sounds very nice."

"Hey," he said, planting a kiss that would linger forever on her lips. "Service is our motto."

* * * * *

Roses are red,
Violets are blue,
Now that we've got a mother,
With mischief we are through.
Casey, Robert and Richard Crawford,
said with almost straight faces.

Roses are red
Violets are blue.
I've never loved before
The way that I love you.
Ryan Crawford

Roses are red,
Violets are blue,
My life is truly complete
Now that I have you.
Valerie Dennison Crawford.

Silhouette Romance®

LONG, TALL TEXANS

**Diana Palmer brings you the
second Award of Excellence title**

SUTTON'S WAY

In Diana Palmer's bestselling Long, Tall Texans trilogy, you
had a mesmerizing glimpse of Quinn Sutton—a mean, lean
Wyoming wildcat of a man, with a disposition to match.

Now, in September, Quinn's back with a story of his own. Set
in the Wyoming wilderness, he learns a few things about women
from snowbound beauty Amanda Callaway—and a lot more
about love.

He's a Texan at heart . . . who soon has a Wyoming wedding in
mind!

The Award of Excellence is given to one specially selected title
per month. Spend September discovering *Sutton's Way*
#670 . . . only in Silhouette Romance.

RS670-1R

COMING SOON...

Indulge a Little
Give a Lot

An irresistible opportunity to pamper
yourself with free* gifts and help a
great cause, Big Brothers/Big Sisters
Programs and Services.

*With proofs-of-purchase plus postage and handling.

Watch for it in October!

Harlequin Books®

Silhouette Books®